short essays by

RALPH BARTHOLDT

Somewhere, Idaho

Ralph Bartholdt's writing and photography have
appeared nationally and in regional publications throughout
the Pacific Northwest. As a reporter he has worked for
news organizations in Washington, Montana and Idaho,
Europe and as an embedded photojournalist with the
1st Marines in Iraq's Anbar Province. His work has been
recognized by the Idaho Press Club, National Newspaper
Association, the Associated Press and the Society of
Professional Journalists. He lives in Idaho's Panhandle.

Acclaim for RALPH BARTHOLDT's

Somewhere, Idaho

"It's gratifying to see someone who can write (this) good ..."
— David E. Petzal, *Field & Stream*

"Bartholdt writes simply, with smarts and passion ... (and) captures his varied topics with a sense of adventure, grace and magic."
— Joe Evancho, author, *FISHING IDAHO - An Angler's Guide*

"Written from experience ... Whimsical, irreverent, humorous, real..."
— Rich Lindsey, *The Idaho Fisherman guide service*

Also by
RALPH BARTHOLDT

Sometime, Idaho

Somewhere, Idaho

RALPH BARTHOLDT

Somewhere, Idaho

ESSAYS

GRASSY MOUNTAIN PRESS
St. Maries, Idaho

For permission requests write to Grassy Mountain Press, grassymountainpress@gmail.com

ISBN: 978-0-578-76710-9 (Paperback)

Library of Congress Control Number: 2020920392

Portions of this book are works of nonfiction. Some of these essays have appeared in *Northwest Sportsman Magazine, The St. Maries Gazette Record, Livingston Enterprise, The Billings Gazette, Missoulian, The Lewiston Tribune* and *Coeur d'Alene Press*.

Photos by Ralph Bartholdt unless otherwise noted.

Book design by Benjamin Riley.

Printed by kdp.amazon.com

First printing edition 2020.

Grassy Mountain Press

Nancy

Contents

Summer

Autumn

Winter

Spring

Summer

Seed Dispersal And A Guy Named Velcro

A burdock plant grows at the edge of my yard in a spot of sun where the dog likes to lay.

It is almost as tall as I am, and its curly leaves are brown like the coat on a retriever.

I could root out the invasive plant, but I don't.

It is a lesson in seed dispersal, and it reminds me of Velcro.

I met Velcro decades ago when I was hanging from a Sitka spruce tree with the steel climbing spurs strapped to my boots precariously slipping from the bark. I wrestled a Skookum brush block with one hand and a steel cable with the other. A Husqvarna chainsaw dangled like an oily pendulum from my belt, threatening to pull me from my perch.

"Need some help?" I heard someone say.

The voice startled me and might have sent me tea-kettling from my aerie except for the wire-core rope that half-hitched me to the trunk.

My mood befouled, I scanned the ground below expecting

an agency official, someone likely from the government marking in a book the transgressions of the occupational safety and health rules in which I was deeply engaged.

I eyed instead a smallish man with frizzy hair springing from beneath a blaze-orange logger's tin hat, not the white, wicker bill helmets emblazoned with government emblems ascribing authority. Government people carried clipboards and a variety of gadgetry dangling from a load-bearing vest. What hung from this man were whiskered jowls and thin arms as he peered lazily up at me.

Sent to the ridge by the boss of the logging show, the man stood in a patch of sun as he considered me with a laconic, owl-like fascination.

He was lean and dressed in the garb of lumberjacks at the time. His rigging jeans were hemless, cut off below the knee barely covering the tops of his high-shaft logging boots. Red suspenders snugged a still-clean railroader shirt tucked inside his trousers and white cotton gloves glowed new, making his hands appear larger than they were. A golf ball bulge of tobacco threatened to jump from his lower lip.

"Looks like you got yourself into a cowcumber," he opined.

The word, not used by anyone anywhere — except the few who had read Lumbering Lingo of the Pacific Northwest — showed he was a philologist and a student of logger talk. He went by the handle Velcro and I got to know him pretty well because we were a small crew and he liked helping me hang rigging blocks from high up in trees. The blocks kept the lines elevated away from the abrasive influence of earth while spryly feeding the ground crew chokers from the sky instead of wrapped, muddily around the haul line.

Velcro volunteered to assist with sundry tasks that prevented exerting himself on the rigging, which is the working end of a high-lead logging show. And he liked to aimlessly chatter, so I learned how he got his name.

Because he was a tramp logger, one whose wanderlust usually kicked in after his second or third payday, Velcro had the opportunity to work in a variety of camps throughout the archipelago and had seen his share of heroics and absurdities.

He left each logging town and lumber camp with a new nickname, something a legal team calls an alias.

In the last camp from which he tramped, Velcro explained, he found himself in the path of impending calamity when a log deck hurled loose from a landing on a hill above him. Without much time to find cover, Velcro slammed himself into the earth as if he were dirt.

A logger who had watched from the safety of a loading machine said in the wake of the thundering logs, the slight, owl-eyed man who stood in the way of the logs as they rained hellfire down the side of the mountain from which they had been previously pulled, had made himself small as a seed pod. Velcro had stuck hard and tight to the ground like a bur.

When the tumult passed, Velcro rose untroubled from the dirt, a little jittery and bark-covered, his eyes still soft and owly, and brushed himself off.

A moniker was born.

Despite appreciating his new-found notoriety, Velcro

gathered his payday and fondness for self-preservation and lit on down the road.

For a while around logging villages of that region, Velcro was only slightly less famous than the hook and loop fastener of the same name developed by a Swiss engineer. It adorns our hunting and fishing gear and is used instead of zippers on everything from jogging pants to magazine pouches.

The product, according to lore, was modeled on burdock seeds that stuck to the fur of the inventor's dog trouncing in the woods.

Back when my hunts were accompanied by sniffing dogs of questionable pedigree, I returned from the field with a shotgun bouncing in the back seat and dogs bouncing along in the front. The dogs and I chewed burs, sticktights, and bramblefidgets from our napes, hocks, socks, and any place we could reach or chew.

It was a delicate business requiring a modicum of dexterity as the car wheeled the curves while its passengers gnawed, spat, and scratched.

On one of those return trips, it dawned on me that I was transporting weeds from far-away fencerows and railroad rights-of-way to my own semi-manicured HOA.

Sticktights are often an inevitable part of the post-bird hunting experience that hunters consider bad luck, reporting "Hanson's wheat patch has got more burdocks than birds."

The Swiss invention inspired by this particular mode of seed dispersal — there are a handful of biotic (read animals) and non-biotic modes such as gravity, wind, and water — is lauded as pretty fair and useful stuff. Grousing is only evinced when accessing the lunch in a Velcro-secured pocket of a backpack while sitting in a tree stand waiting for a stealthy whitetail. We compare the ripping sound to a Cape Canaveral launch but deer don't seem to mind it any more than popping brush, or the smell of wood smoke.

Unlike his name suggested, the owl-like man with frizzy hair didn't stick around our camp too long. His tendency to grow on you was offset by the restlessness that eventually dispersed him elsewhere.

The burdock, lean and bristly at the edge of the yard is, for now, a fixture that will remain until its seeds are carried off and the slim stalk dislodged.

It's this addiction to movement and to grow temporary roots that reminds me of Velcro, or whatever his handle these days.

Forget The Shotgun, Get A Fly Rod Holder

Windshield wipers are made for bugs and dust.

In a more perfect world, the wipers work hand in hand with fluid that is part detergent and part streak-free glass cleaner, or at least a relative of both.

If it's a clean windshield you're after, a slosh of water works in a pinch.

Unless it's rainwater and your fly rods are being held in place by the wipers as you drive.

In that case, things won't work out for you.

I had a No. 4 Orvis that was light as the tailfeather of a rooster pheasant. It shared an ochre hue with roasted chestnuts and laid an iridescent midge pattern so delicately on water dappled by sipping fish that shedding a tear was expected.

When they witnessed this phenomenon, fellow anglers stopped to hold their ball caps over their hearts.

"Oops," my buddy said one day as we headed upriver. The

sky which had been sunny one moment, darkened and cut loose the next.

Raindrops like spitballs popped on the hood where the rusty wiper arms and their half-hearted blades, sun-and-ice-chewed from years of misuse, held our fly rods snugly against the windshield.

When my pal snapped on the wipers the fly rods went in different directions, but mostly overboard.

He turned to me and grinned like a seller of used cars who swallowed a gob of chewing gum.

"Shouldn'ta done that," he said.

"Prolly not," I replied.

And we backtracked.

The rods were fine.

They were just a little scuffed from the pavement, which was already drying as the sun again came out. Bugs now swarmed from the water as if the cloudburst provided a new incentive for them to get out there and dance.

It wasn't long after that my pal snapped the tip off the Orvis with a car door.

It was my fault, however, and I told him so.

"Don't worry about it," I said.

And then I grieved.

It was on another trip, the same river when a fill-in fly rod took the heat. This time a slight drizzle prompted the inadvertent flip of the windshield wiper switch.

"Oops," my pal said. "I keep doing that."

We backtracked and found the fly rods. One was without a

tip, but we fished with it anyhow.

Streamer chucking or fly hurling doesn't have to be pretty and often — as on that day — it isn't.

It was for this reason that I sat in a lawn chair all afternoon in the sweltering driveway last month waiting for the delivery van.

I waited for the arrival of one of the greatest inventions of all time.

It wasn't American-made, but the fact gave me little pause.

The brainy contraption was conceived in the land of sea trout, the infamous *Salmo trutta*. These are sea-run browns so surly it takes a pint, maybe two, to fully wrap one's head around the concept of their intrepidity.

My new rod holders with magnetic strips that kept them clinging to a car hood, and fine elastic straps that cinched both rod and cork, hailed from Wales.

Great Britain that is. The home of the wet fly swing, peat-tinged water, and the foamy head.

I expected Old World craft, and I expected it soon.

The ratty lawn chair was getting the best of me as I sat with shades on, wearing short pants, dangling a flip flop on the end of an untanned foot that draped over a knee.

I had tracked the package and it was on its way.

To my house.

No more relying on $12 wiper blades to hold fly rods that cost more than that.

No more driving through downpours gritting one's teeth as hands flinched, or moved haltingly toward the wiper knob.

No white knuckle shouts from passengers during a gully washer — "For Gawdsake! Slow down! I can't see!" — while racing with a head out the window to the next fishing hole.

Nuh-uh.

So when the delivery van drove up, I casually strolled over. I was jittery as a pointer pup, full of adrenaline and anticipation.

"How's it going?" I asked.

The question was rhetorical.

The man rummaged in the back of the van.

Then he rummaged some more. I heard boxes being tossed and a long sigh.

Then he came forward, sat in the driver seat of the toaster-shaped van with its open, sliding door and reliable emblem, and with hands on his thighs said, "I got nothing."

He reached for the ignition.

"Wait," I said, grabbing the door handle. "Yes, you do."

My teeth chattered and my knees started to knock. I felt my back hunch, hyena-like.

He sensed my urgency.

"What you expecting?" He asked.

"Fly rod holder," I barely knit the words together. "It is supposed to be here today."

"You're going fishing?"

I nodded and uttered the sacred words, "A week on the river."

He knew then.

The delivery man wearing shorts and a pressed shirt had been rigid and straight-backed in the high spring seat. His two hands had moved to the steering wheel and now, with elbows locked, he turned to me. His gaze bored into my pupils. Almost trancelike he killed the engine and slipped slowly from his chair to once again rummage in the back of the van, tossing boxes, shuffling.

Then silence, followed by another, deeper sigh.

A minute later he returned and handed a battered package — all the way from Wales — through the door to me.

"Sorry I couldn't find it earlier," he said. "Summer help never puts things in their place."

I recognized the faint and distant peal of bells.

"Thank you," I said.

"Good luck fishing," the man said as the engine growled to life.

Before accelerating, he paused.

We shared a requiem for broken fly rod tips, rain showers, bugs, and dust: The hardships, pent eagerness, and challenges overcome to drop an imitation bug on slick and soundless water.

He nodded once, then drove away leaving me standing in a cloud of exhaust gazing skyward with my ball cap held over my heart.

Then I bolted into the garage to slap the holder to my hood and fit it with a brace of beat-up fly rods.

SOMEWHERE, IDAHO

Meaty Memories

It's true. I fired up the barbecue last weekend.

"It's true," is an affirmation, because I imagine the annual ritual may have been publicized like a party line.

The neighbors likely ratted me out.

They didn't call the fire department this time, although I surmise at least one of them was poised behind a window curtain with the speed dial.

It may have been Jimmy who thinks I have forgotten to replace his cedar fence, and likely wonders when the hair on his cat will grow back.

Even if word spread through the HOA like a gasoline fire — no one ever puts lighter fluid on the shopping list — last weekend's grill fest was worth every windblown ember. Succulence and charbroil were smeared across the face of all who partook of the tenderloin.

Tenderloin is a misnomer for a piece of meat that, expertly fire-charred, kindles memories of yule logs, those aromatic pieces of Christmas lumber whose soot sullies the wallpaper and raises the fire alarms.

Last weekend's cuts notwithstanding, everyone who banqueted walked away with a charcoal smile because I gracefully cured the cuts with coal and heat, not unlike the stuff you get at the good truck stops.

Overlook for a moment the grass stuck to choice cuts — the lawn is a good place to extinguish burning meat — and it's evident my prowess with flames and chops goes back a ways.

Among the choicest protein I've ever fire-cooked is muskrat.

The idea to serve up a plate of yellow-toothed, beady-eyed stew meat on a stick marinated during a late-autumn camping trip before it reached full-on cuisine.

My pal Boggsy and I struck upon the notion at the same time as we navigated a sinewy northern waterway.

We both said it aloud, mid-paddle stroke, then grinned as if what passed between us had been a Eureka moment.

We'd been canoeing much of the day on a black stream in a mostly roadless section of outback where the muskrats we didn't catch in our trapline were plugged with the crack of a .22 rifle from the wicker seat of the canoe.

The day was presaged with hoarfrost and we took our time sliding on water as slick as oil skin because we knew back at camp there was no shortage of sardines, beans, and bricks of noodles — all the epicurean delights that historically, over a century of woodsmanship, have kept statesmen luxuriously idling in camp.

We had no sherry or cognac in artfully designed bottles, but somewhere stashed away was a pint of peppermint schnapps.

Red meat was sorely extinct from the lockbox where we kept the stores. And then Boggsy held up a skinned rat by its rubbery tail as the tip of his paddle dripped, and asked, "What if?"

Say no more.

After a day checking traps, we returned to our camp on a granite swale surrounded by stunted spruce, pulled the canoe to its moorings, and sparked a fire before skinning, then skewering rats on a stick.

Muskrat meat, for the uninitiated, can cure scurvy and a sweet tooth at the same time. The hide is good for ear muffs, so there's that, as a salesman friend often says.

A good muskrat hock is a sirloin all over again, but who would have believed it? Charred outside like a marshmallow, the inside is blissful pink, loin-like, and tender as a hummingbird's breast.

I go back there a lot when I grill, to that time, late fall, in the canoe Up North with bluebills setting their wings, shooting through the black spruce and tamarack sloughs as if on a zipline.

The water was cold and dark as we dipped our paddles then watched the drips from them make rings behind us like orbits of a spinning planet.

Sometimes I wonder if it was as first-rate as I make it now, with so much time etherized and hurried into the atmosphere.

Memories are like zucchini. They grow big and beautiful

but are hard to get rid of, so I often regard what I remember of muskrat meat with suspicion.

I would try it again, given the chance. Maybe with less youthful exuberance than on that weeklong trip decades ago in the border country when we, as myopic kids, packed a minimal cache of calories into our canoe before pushing off.

For now, I say c'est la vie and know those words aren't homonyms.

I'm grilling.

Chicken, beef, pork, throw on a muskrat if you got it.

It's the charcoal season when Pepto Bismol is as good a condiment as sauce, and neighbors keep their cell phones handy.

"Grab the gas can from the garage, son. These coals need a spurt!"

Muster Up A Hammock Tent

My children found a colorful, semi-neon, fully insect-proof hammock tent in an outdoor catalog and were utterly delighted.

It was called an air dome, but other varieties had different names.

"Like, who thought of that?" one of them shrilled. "It's a tent and a hammock in one! You hang it, crawl in, and zip it up. If it rains you don't get wet ... Bugs? Gone!"

"Fascinating," I replied remembering the olive green hammock tent my family found in the attic when I was a kid.

The kids' catalog tent was a spanking, newly-marketed version while mine, way back when, had been left behind by previous owners along with an American flag missing two stars, and a pair of knee-high riding boots without jodhpurs.

My dad dragged the tent into the yard like an archeological find and the neighbor kids came over to poke it with sticks.

"What is it?" One of them asked.

Another grownup standing nearby explained its history as once-standard equipment of jungle wars. Burma, he said, Marawi, the Golden Triangle.

His musing as he stood with the sleeves of his Madras shirt rolled up on his forearms while puffing a MacArthur pipe stoked our imaginations.

We stomped on the tent to kill spiders as big as Susan B. Anthonys that were mostly already dead, their crinkly carapaces clung to tent corners like tiny zombies. Then we snaked the garden hose out into the yard and sprayed the tent until it stuck to the ground like flypaper. We hung it over three clotheslines, but that didn't get rid of the mildew smell, which to this day reminds me of the bear and the crow.

After we dragged the hammock tent to a grove of pines on the sunset side of the yard, we tied its lanyards to branches as high as we could reach using knots that required a pocket knife to undo.

And there it hung.

Just like that.

Hammock tent. Rubberized skin flaking in places, its mesh a foggy breath. It aired out for a week as we waited to muster the courage to overcome our fear of spiders, scurrying silverfish, pincer-mouth centipedes, and bats we believed must call the tent home. Any ghosts that nested all those years as the tent lay balled in the attic had been given adequate time to flee.

As a sort of christening and to serve as bait, someone eventually had to climb inside.

Being the youngest, I was fortunate to be granted opportunities like this. As I lay in the tent with the zippers zipped, neighbor kids watched from a distance.

They anticipated commotion, screams, ghouls vacating the premises like green smoke, and possibly the arrival of an ambulance.

I fell asleep.

I was tired a lot back then as I recall because of the sun, and the lake we plunged into from the end of the dock, and because of endlessly chasing stuff like other people's arrows and baseballs, and baby ducks. Or, being chased by stuff like yellow jackets, sticks, dogs, and that one bear.

The bear, in hindsight, didn't chase me. But when I woke from one of my sojourns in the hammock tent, there it was. Not a large black bear, probably a yearling roaming and getting into trouble — just like the neighborhood kids.

I felt a kinship, but at the same time it was a bear and I had been taught to not trust them.

We all knew from watching television that angry bears stand on their hind legs and growl and bite. It was apparent even to me, that a black bear of this size could, if he were mad or hungry, consider the hammock tent with me inside as easy cuisine.

When the bear turned its back in favor of a chokecherry bush, I unzipped, dropped to the ground, and ran.

Shocked by my presence mere feet away, the bear scampered just as fast in another direction.

He was seen belly deep in a trash can at a neighbor's place

down the road the next day, and an angler said he spotted the bear swimming across the lake to Ely Island where blueberries ripened.

The baby crow came later. We found it flightless under one of the pines and as all budding naturalists, we felt it our duty to take the squabbling barely-feathered lizard home and feed it canned dog food.

It didn't appear to like us much. It pecked and cawed and when we had it outside in a shoebox its calling attracted other crows that seemed to scold us from the limbs of surrounding trees. We kept it behind the netting of the hammock tent safe from cats and other unpleasantries. That is where its mom watched as we fed and watered it before it died.

A sorrowful few minutes followed the discovery of the ugly little bird that had barely fledged, and we mourned its demise.

Then we forgot about it — leaving the lifeless entity to fester in the hammock tent because no one wanted to touch its carcass. We committed to providing it a proper burial, eventually, and moved on to other endeavors.

During the dog days of summer, we kept away from the plastic humidity of the hammock tent as it hung between two trees, stretched out, empty except for the dead bird and spiders, its mildewy essence a mere memory.

In the meantime someone, a parent perhaps, had flicked the baby crow carcass with its squiggly fly worms into the underbrush. The neighbor kids and I, by the end of summer, rediscovered the hammock tent that by now had become a fixture, almost unnoticed until we climbed back inside.

We lay in the sump of the canvas one more time as the sun set behind trees. We imagined bears and crows and spiders and wondered how the heck mosquitoes continued to find their way inside given all the zippers and netting and stuff.

I don't know what happened to that hammock tent. It was for one summer a novelty despite its lack of neon or a rousing, otherworldly name.

When my children asked can we get one? I said sure, but only from the military surplus store.

For the price of a new hammock tent, a traveler could, with a decent currency exchange rate, buy airfare and a lengthy stay at an Albanian youth hostel.

Money doesn't grow on trees, after all, I said rolling up the sleeves on my flannel, button-front shirt. It's good to know, however, that some memories do.

SOMEWHERE, IDAHO

A Good Hat Is Hard To Find

Ron Meek and I stood on the banks of Boulder River near Big Timber and watched a jet boat the size of a Florida shrimper power up the roiling water that dumped from the Absaroka Range into the Yellowstone.

The Boulder is a rocky stream with silver water pounding large, washed stones, and the boat's gunwales could have notched the trees on both sides.

On her bow was a bikini blond in Farrah sunglasses and the man behind the wheel sported gelled hair and a serious "uh-oh" look as if he had taken a wrong turn in his quest for the Yellowstone Club.

Meek, a lanky fly fishing guide in his mid-50s with a beard going gray and eyes that said he's seen his share of asininities, looked at me and smiled.

Holding his 9-foot, 5-weight fly rod, he mouthed something but the words were lost in the weight of the engine's roar.

After the boat came back down and its noise disappeared,

we settled in for some nymphing and he told of guiding Sandra Day O'Connor in Mongolia, and how the then-Supreme Court justice took him to task for misidentifying a taimen.

"That's a rainbow, Ron," she told him. "I have caught a lot of fish and I know a rainbow when I see one."

Meek, who falls asleep counting trout of all makes and models, agreed with her.

There was no reason not to.

"I'm a humble man," he said.

He gave me a yellow hat with the name of the guide school that prompted me to drive that far east over the Great Divide to fish for trout.

He taught me how to make indicators out of yarn and small rubber bands, how a river ticket (toilet paper) was something you couldn't use twice, and how, when it comes to fishing, ignorance can sometimes be the mother of keen invention.

We caught rainbow trout that day as shiny as a cutlass.

I have used what he showed on several rivers for several years, often while wearing the yellow hat, which became nicely sun-faded and form-fitted.

Last week on the interstate heading to a new trout haunt — one that I was assured was severely underfished and little known — the yellow hat leaped from my head and spun behind me on the asphalt.

Several semi-trucks and the usual vacationing throng of traveling families in minivans, SUVs, and Winnebagos bore down on it.

I watched it disappear in the rearview. I wanted to stop, but danger said no.

There were other reasons.

My instincts told me to keep driving. It was time to let go. To move on. To wear one of the other hats that I keep in a backpack and don't wear for reasons I've never addressed.

Despite the fine fishing at the new spot, which required a long trek on a two-track over federal land that seemed ideal for the cacti that grew there, I couldn't stop thinking about the hat.

"It's just a hat," someone said. "I'll buy you another."

It's true, but I looked for it anyhow on the way back without sighting it.

It's just a hat, I told myself. A material thing. Who cares?

It was identical to one that Tracy Peterson of the Umpqua school wore on the Yellowstone when he told me to run the drift boat straight through a gauntlet of rocks that had a rainbow of spray on the other side and a wall of foam for an encore.

"I came through that once," he said after we made it to soft water. "I stuck the nose of the boat straight down and capsized."

He grinned.

Memories like that, the love of the sport and that particular summer, prodded me to go back looking for the sun-bleached cover.

The next morning as dew kept down the dust and the sun barely crested a butte, I rolled up the highway and instead of heading home, I took a detour.

I counted pronghorns above what's become a familiar river. I saw my hat kicked in the sage and I stopped.

I walked across the four-lane highway and listened to a meadowlark. Glanced the flickering tail of a deer. I picked up the hat and set it on.

Good hats are hard to find, I said aloud to no one.

Then I returned to the pickup truck, slammed the door, cut across the grassy median, and trundled west to home.

That Road Will Take You Anywhere

We found a secret fishing spot.

It was over the mountains and down some narrow roads where meeting another vehicle heading the other way could spell disaster.

It was an hour from town through a slate-colored morning, so we stopped at the Tesoro station for coffee in paper cups. The attendant waited for her replacement. Her hair revealed the sheen of someone up all night and her eyes said who cares.

We drove around the golf course at the edge of the lake where the lawn guys fired up the mowers before the first tee-time. Then we headed into the hills on switchback roads made for logging trucks before the federal government decided lost tax revenue and letting forests die on the hill by beetles and mismanagement was a fine alternative to providing jobs and income to pay for libraries, schools and box lunches.

The new policy said it's better to go bust than bump knots.

We sped along empty forest roads built by timber dollars

that were once meticulously maintained by loggers charged with road care. The roads now are used for recreation instead of log hauling and the lack of a tax base makes maintenance sketchy. At an even twenty miles per hour we sent dirt and muck flying from chuck holes, skirted caved road banks and thumped over erosion rills in our efforts to get to the stream we called the honey hole.

Secret fishing spots are nothing more than places others haven't visited in a while. They may be at the end of a trail or just far enough around a brushy bend to make getting there onerous. They have been fished, but not this week, or last, for that matter, or maybe in a month or more.

They are places where ethics have played their part, where anglers have done what their conscience has asked of them: pack it in, pack it out, catch and release, and leave no trace.

Those are the three commandments of backwoods, westslope cutthroat trout fishing and we have all, at one time or another, sought repentance for angling against them; maybe in our back pages, because of youthful ignorance, lust, greed, or bliss.

At this hole, a sweet spot with a long narrow run pressing against a bank under a river birch and gurgling past a series of rock outcroppings, a halcyon pool curled like cream stout and deep as a copper pot. Earlier in the season we caught cutthroat trout here of forearm length and thickness. That is why we once again choked down the coffee from the Tesoro station that tasted like cigarette butts, scratched the grist on our faces and called in sick.

It was why we came back.

We had cast at the upstream riffle where the water rushed into a pool and ran out just as fast. The trout there flashed full-body chasing the fly and the ones we hooked were heavy as truncheons when we dragged them through the frigid water to shore after they were spent.

The fish were golden with black spots on the tail like an hourglass set upright, or as if the fish had been fighting hard currents that squeezed the spots down sleek bodies like pebbles in a bottleneck. Red gill flares gave them their name.

One, a cutthroat trout of sixteen inches or more was scarred on the dorsi. It seemed to grin nonetheless when we let it fin back into the dark pool under craggy basalt.

We returned to this spot many times as the water warmed, before the woods filled up for the summer holidays.

An old-timer we knew who had packed a .45 around Europe when the world wasn't weary enough for another war, and who lived most of his summer days in those mountains chasing trout in waters few had tested with a fly, said he always left the forest before the holidays.

"I don't know why people have to go to the mountains to drink," he said.

He returned afterward when the camp trailers were gone.

We followed the routine, and now with the holiday weekend over we drained our coffee somewhere around the second or third intersection where one lonely gravel strip met another as the day dawned gray then white. It foretold heat and we anticipated morning sunlight dappling stream banks.

We found our secret spot had tire tracks busting through syringa and ocean spray.

A campfire ring was broad and cold under a cedar. In its ash were charred cans of gas station beers, crumpled and drained. Fish vertebrae with translucent speckled skins and tails still intact were heat-glued to a rock.

The streamside too had an air of a kid whose bail you posted.

ATVs had spat rocks, dug trenches, trampled mint, and fireweed. Bobbers and barbed hooks hung from the river birch over the current running dark, where the fat fish earlier that summer launched for flies.

We cast for an hour without a take or a rise.

A while later we hooked a mid-range cutthroat and let it go. We changed flies, used droppers, streamers, and small surface bugs. The fish were mostly gone.

Interlopers out for a holiday in the burly woods with all their toys and embellishments had sucked the sweetness from that mountain stream.

According to a report by Idaho Fish and Game published before cutthroat trout was a catch and release species in Idaho's Panhandle, more bigger fish were the inevitable result of limited harvest. Also, most anglers wanted restrictive regulations for cutthroat trout if it resulted in a better fishery, and a few anglers (35%) in the 1978 study wanted streams "closed" altogether.

In a 2005 study after catch and release regulations had been adopted for several years on the St. Joe River, state fishery biologists concluded, "Appreciable numbers of cutthroat trout in the 12-inch-plus range were not observed in the St. Joe River until the regulations were set to catch-and-release."

The panhandle's catch and release rules for cutthroat trout have resulted in a fatter and better fishery in the two main raiver drainages where catch and release is the modus operandi.

Westslope cutthroat trout are a native Idaho species. Unlike trout in many put-and-take fisheries, these fish have genetics fostered in the same streams they fin today; spiraling alpha-helixes imprinted with tributaries, springs, and the acidity of undercut banks their ancestors knew for centuries. Catching a cutthroat in one of North Idaho's streams and checking its markings — spots mostly near the tail with little spotting below the lateral line — is something we don't appreciate until we catch what biologists consider a real westslope. Many of the cutts previously caught showed enough rainbow trout characteristics to indicate they were the progeny of mixed genetics and named for it. We call them cuttbows.

The fish we caught and released before the July holiday in our one-time secret spot were all pure strain westslope cutthroat trout named for the region they inhabit west of the Continental Divide. They were beauties with bloodlines of significance that should have excluded them as the main ingredient in campfire hash.

There are many streams where an angler can hook and

keep a pot full of brookies. Brook trout may be had by the bucketful with a limit of twenty five fish. Not long ago we found a brook trout stream and brought home a half dozen of the colorful square-tails for the broiler. Rainbows can be kept too, as part of a combined trout limit of six, where applicable.

The state fishery department hasn't dumped rainbows into North Idaho streams for decades because they were shaving the gene pool of its westslope population, but native bows are still found in some northern Idaho watersheds.

To illegally use worms and barbed hooks to catch native trout and have them smoke in a fire pit is doltish and dishonest, and for anyone who likes catching wild fish over again, it's a dilemma.

The state of the river that day left us with little to say, so we pressed the windshield wiper blades against our fly rods to keep them strapped tight to the glass, and drove home.

Next spring, before the summer holidays, before the bait and barbed hook bandits rob the undercut banks we will revisit the secret spot to learn what new fish have moved in.

We will re-establish the routine that banks on goodness while it lasts, and realizes someone's hallowed ground is another's camp hash.

We'll apply carpe diem to fly fishing.

It's the deal you make with the future; a diplomacy that anticipates another day.

Let's Forget About High Mountain Lakes

A friend who introduced me to custom firearms and the Idaho backcountry in winter, both of them accessible to anyone with a passion for either, once harvested a mountain goat, sliding the billy down to a high mountain lake where he camped.

He dressed and cooked some of the meat on a fire, he said, carefully tending the memory of the occasion as one worth keeping.

He recounted it down to the color of his socks and the bindings of the snowshoes he carried.

There was a problem, however. He could never again find the mountain lake.

It was surrounded by trees, and the goat slid easily on the snow because the incline was steep, and it was a good place for an overnight camp under a sky full of stars as thick as a mohair coat.

The lake, though, seemed to have fallen off the map.

"I never did know the name of it," he said.

Mountain lakes can be like that. Sometimes you almost stumble upon and fall into them, and at other times you know where they are by an app, but finding them on foot is another affair altogether.

Dan Mottern at the fly shop in Avery has hiked his share of mountain trails, and he has pedaled and carried his bicycle to peaks in the St. Joe forest that have no trails — or what remains of the trails is just a whiff of a once vibrant national forest trail maintenance program.

He knows his way around the saddles and ridges and pinnacles as well as anyone, but there was that time when he and his daughters bushwhacked to a lake that was pretty close to a road, but without trail access.

"We missed it," he said.

It was late afternoon. Business at the fly shop had dropped off and he decided to gather a child or two and head out to fish a mountain lake he had eyed for a few years, but not visited.

He and his co-pilots used dead reckoning, and the landmarks they remembered from Google Earth, as summer daylight dwindled.

Despite a good try, he still hasn't been to the lake he knows is out there, and that, according to the whispered accounts, holds sizable grayling.

A man in Lewiston who hunted the same area for elk hasn't been there either.

"I never could find that lake," he said.

It is less than a mile from a fairly heavily traveled back

road but its tree-covered bowl hides in terrain as lumpy as truckstop oatmeal.

There are treasures to be found on a bushwhack, and a lot of magnificent nooks you mark by memory and will never visit again. But if you're hiking to a lake to fish, it's better to get there.

That's why we often stick to the well-worn trails.

They are broad and tramped out and usually visible even under a canopy of large fir at night.

The hangup for a hermit-like hiker on a journey of self-discovery is that people use these trails, so wherever they lead you'll probably have company. Which could mean you may spend a night camped along shore humming along to someone else's campfire song, or nodding off to the late-evening, confidential and wine-addled tales from a few members of a midlife club.

Arriving early at the trailhead and hiking briskly to a high mountain lake doesn't ensure solitude. You might as well just settle in and listen to the voices that carry across high mountain lakes like a radio with the volume stuck on clear.

"Did you step in that? You stepped in that! You gotta be careful where you're walkin,' bro."

Up there in the higher country, the elevation is the limiting factor.

Hiking to a high-mountain lake reminds you of what you did too much, or too little in the weeks leading up to the hike.

Stops aren't called beer or smoke breaks. They are barely called anything at all. But "cinwetakeabreather?" or "yougotwater?," may presage a wheeze.

Some of the best hikes are uphill both ways and even if you don't return to relive the adventure, the trail's end sticks to your memory for its mission and its accomplishment.

You always remember the fish that appear more colorful so close to the sun. They are stout. Invariably hungry. Wild on the line.

And you recall the steps like climbing into the sky and returning to earth.

All of this however is relished much later because sometimes while hiking to a high mountain lake what you miss most is the comfort of level ground.

Trolling For Truth, Casting For Cause

Let me tell you about my Uncle Jim.

He is a walleye fisherman. There was a time when he fished brook trout in streams the banks of which were so thick with willow and dog-hair spruce that sun shafts barely colored the water.

The streams ran cold and black, the bugs in them fat as chub minnows, and the trout, when held in cracks of daylight, dripped rainbows from their glistening scales.

"That's a young man's game, that trout fishing," my Uncle Jim said. "You need the legs for it."

At 82 years old, his legs were better suited for tending to the tomatoes he grew in carts that he wheeled around his lakeside yard, parking them in the warm blotches of sunshine falling through the trees.

His legs were better suited, too, for walleye. Those you catch while seated in an 18-foot Lund, with one eye on the depth finder and another on the rod tip as the outboard chugs evenly, keeping the bow pointed into a steady chop.

Jim fished for walleyes in the same lake so long that he can feel his way home at night from Big Bay without running lights. He pushed straight two miles toward the black hump of the mainland, arced around the reef at Birch Island and cut a silver wake through the narrows without dropping speed before s-curving around the buoys that bobbed silently in the light from a snippet of moon and the stars.

He didn't slow until he motored into the paddies at the edge of the bay where he lived in a remodeled cabin with his wife, Phyllis, and the photos of their daughter and son-in-law and the many hunting dogs they have raised through the years.

He was fishing the same lake when Herbert Hoover was president. He walked a path from town to Pike Bay to wet a line the year Jack Sharkey defeated Max Schmeling in New York City, the year Knut Rockne died, the year the Lindbergh baby was kidnapped.

My Uncle Jim was in the army in the North Pacific during The Big One.

Afterward, he returned to his hometown and the lake.

He saw the local ore mine boom and die and the people pack up and move out.

He could have purchased all of Puncher Point for pocket change when the owner approached him with the deal more than fifty years ago but didn't. No money.

Others, years later, took advantage.

Shoulder to shoulder, their million-dollar homes line the point now. They are summer residents with planes and two-engine tri-hulls.

A paved road painted with yellow and white lines, glistening as if freshly scrubbed, has buried the path to Pike Bay that my Uncle Jim once walked.

Having spent so much time tied indelibly to a lake that shimmers in summer's moonlight, and cracks and groans beneath the northern lights of winter imbued him with a certain sharpness like a shard of light glancing from a wave tip, or an ice-chip.

The point of his wit was directed, invariably, at the self-righteous and self-important.

It was often directed at newspapers and those who wrote them and steered their editorial pages.

Unusual perhaps, given that my Uncle Jim was a newspaperman for a great part of his life.

Although he sold The Tower News and its antiquated printing press and linotype long ago he honed the clarity and sharpness of a newspaperman still.

Once each summer when I knocked on his screen door and he waved me in with an arm and a grin to the living room and its duck prints, memories, and a dog wagging a heavy tail, he related to me the news of the past year as he knew it.

Frankly. Concisely. Eloquently.

Lastly, came the opinion pieces. He announced them beforehand to certify that they were not news, but his mind.

When I responded with my new-day-and-age newspaper philosophy that pretended to reveal, he pined.

He replied with a story of a gray wolf that was shot on an island one winter. Everybody in his small town of five hundred inhabitants knew the perpetrator, he supposed. A ruckus was raised by the urban news stations, and federal agents drove out and stomped around and the hoopla, he said, didn't die down until the ice broke up and the docks were lowered into the water and the talk turned to walleye, or muskies and bass.

The wolf killer was not meted out.

Wolves have plied that lake country as long as anyone can remember, and just as long they have been put down not for sport as much as to protect a livelihood or a life, and for purposes of management.

Laws sometimes, and judge's decrees, are often injudicious and injurious and worth less than the paper they are printed on.

What he meant was that some things are relative and some aren't. Some things die natural deaths and some don't. Sometimes truth reflects climate and longitude, but not politics, not ever, and in the end should come the opinion pieces. They should be announced beforehand to certify they are not news but thoughts on a matter, however enlightened, caustic, or unpopular. However priggish or out to lunch.

They are not stymied or stifled or kicked out or in and they do not share the same habitat with matters of fact.

They are all, however, purposeful and worth considering because they are the ingredients that make the chowder served up in communities across the country. By the bowl or spoonful — or not accepted at all — they aim to nourish or supplement whatever it is we think we know, or we don't, and that's it.

Aside from one walleye spot in particular that my Uncle Jim showed me decades ago, I want to remember that above all things.

Autumn

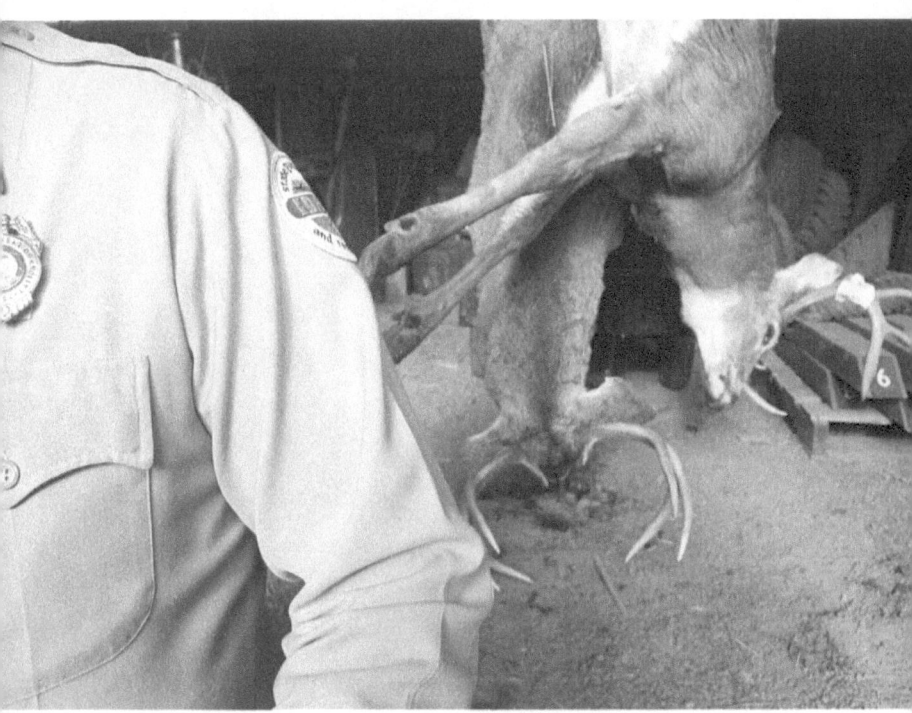

Tracking Night Into Day

It doesn't get any more natural than this.

Everything out here is organic.

You're walking a trail that your pupils, wide as dimes, can barely make using shards of light scraped from the night.

Your learning started fifteen minutes ago, the time it took to get the gear together from the back seat and carry it through the chill across the dirt patch of road to the trailhead. From there you trudged up the path a hundred feet, two hundred feet and then you stopped and listened. You adjusted your bow and your backpack. Checked manually for things like binoculars, knives, bull elk and cow calls, and camo gloves, the gear you've learned to pack while keeping the junk to a minimum.

You checked for these by feel because it's dark as the inside of a cedar box and your hands are cold as you wait for your eyes to adjust to the night like a cat, and for your pupils to crank open like a can of soup.

In the meantime, you listened for the distant engines of other hunters heading your way so early this morning, and also for the thin, taut bugles of bull elk wafting from timber canyons like wind-borne spider webs. So faint, curling, lifting, falling, but you didn't hear any of it.

No rattle-bang of a pickup truck echoed from a mountainside after being muffled in a creek bottom before clambering from a washboard road like the pounding of a belt gun.

Not yet.

You wear three shirts but will shed one soon after you cut a sweat.

On the trail a squeaking, squealing sound stops you. It means the morning breeze has started squirreling in the poke-pole tops of snags, the ones that rub against standing green trees and the rubbing of the wood is eerie as a slate call.

But it's natural and not unusual. There is the sound of the wind now too in the brushy tops of pine and fir, a wooing sound, ghoulish that ends in a hush.

It's been a while since you heard and recognized the sounds that now come back like old pals who want to scare the bejesus out of you and later laugh about it.

You remove a shirt, roll it tight, and push it into a side pocket of your cargo pants before shuffling up the trail, gaining elevation.

A loud bump and the clatter of stones and then a wheezing huff make you freeze for a moment. A louder huff and then more stomping follows.

Deer. They bound downslope away from you breaking limbs and brush.

You give it a rest. You're breathing hard and so are the doe and her fawns, as they wonder about you. You wait until the deer trail off.

You're gaining elevation and check your watch. Another half-hour to the ridge and then another thirty minutes you surmise to the big draw that angles downhill to the park. The vague metallic light that falls around you is accompanied by the mewing sound of a raven somewhere in the trees. Then the wing pumping swoosh, swoosh, swoosh as the big bird trails you from overhead to get a better look. It lights on a high limb making a bell sound. All's OK. Just a hunter heading to the place the elk herd slid over the saddle last night, it seems to say, and another raven perched at a higher elevation mews in return. The call mimics a cow elk. The two birds do this for a minute and then you hear them push off. Their wingbeats fade down the reach to the valley where through the trees you see the silhouette of the neighboring mountain that you'll use as a bearing in the daylight.

Trees squeak in the breeze like yawning hinges. A squirrel skitters up a trunk, its claws scratches the bark, and it chirps.

You're two miles above the trailhead and now, intermittently stopping, you hear an engine accelerate and coast around a turn far below you. The diesel rattles and its cylinders clunk up into the sky through a mist you just now notice. The sky is lighting and you smell the barnyard whiff of livestock, but out here it's elk. They mucked along in the elderberries hours earlier and left behind their hoof prints in the dust where they crossed the path, noticeable by starlight. In the stiff air, their scent lingers.

Browsed stems glow in the darkness like candle wax, branches and pedicles peeled, chewed, and spit out.

After hiking more than an hour, you clamor up and out of the saddle carrying in one hand your bow by the strings because it's almost shooting light and you have folded the carrying strap into another side pocket of your pants.

As you hike higher one step at a time the organic noises of the night mix with crepuscular sounds, normal renderings of the morning, and the lingering whiff of elk, breeze blown, again criss-crosses your path. It swirls around.

Through the trees, miles away, you see a rural valley and the last flickering of yard lights.

You stop for a break and to breathe.

A put-put-put sound seems almost at your feet.

Then an explosion stops your heart for a brief moment. Ruffed grouse. Its blurring wings hop over a ridge and through the trees carrying with it the bird you failed to notice before your nearness frightened it to flight, and it frightened you.

Now you are past the side hill to the benches and the open trees under a dark canopy where you stop. Wipe away the sweat. Listen.

Three miles from the trailhead, maybe more, the nearest road is the one you left.

You'll wait here for the wind to change or for the high notes of a bugle to whinny through the trees followed by a chuckle.

Your sweat cools and dries. A shiver of cold climbs your neck.

Then.

There it is.

A bull elk squeals through the dawn from what may be a finger ridge to the west.

Then a separate call from a different approach, that one closer.

How many yards away? You measure what you think you know about sound and distance.

From a shirt pocket you lift a diaphragm call as big as a half dollar, place it on your tongue and adjust it.

You decide to move through the shadowy morning when the bulls bugle again, to mask your footfalls and to get a bearing.

Dead reckoning.

You'll jog in their direction through the half-light as they call, and stop, kneeling in shadows when they pause their calling.

You'll do it again, returning a mew sound with the diaphragm call you roll on your tongue like a lozenge.

When you stop, you listen.

You're looking for ambush sites.

Your senses are jazzed.

Open Land Idaho

Like feathered corkscrews, the brace of grouse flew straight up through a funnel of pine toward a patch of blue sky, and we raised our guns, Honer and me, knocking the birds to the ground.

They plopped in the needle duff between us, flurrying their wings, as ruffed grouse are prone until their brains said you're dead, and we knew we had muffed it.

The thunderous shots from our too-big guns would surely alert the landowner who we watched earlier from behind the cover of pines as he sidled on horseback, not a half-mile away over his section of land.

We were kids hoisting twelve gauge, three inch magnum, hardware-store fowling pieces, trailing an assortment of mongrel pointing or flushing dogs as we sneaked every weekend onto fenced ranch land, privately owned. This is where we lured ducks and geese using wooden mouth calls, and flushed grouse on the wide-open and rolling ground we deemed our own. We carried slugs in our back pockets for deer, in the event necessity demanded we harvest a buck that only the best of fortune had placed in front of our beaded shotgun sites.

We had done this for many weeks each autumn for a few years without incident but now, there he was with an entourage, the landowner seated on a bay with flared nostrils. Saddles squeaked as his guests shared a moment of piety while looking down from their high perches at Honer and me and the birds we hung from our belts.

Our guns faintly smoked.

Red handed, as they say, is what we were.

The landowner was a businessman whose nationally-known company had its headquarters in the city, and he looked us over and asked how we had come to be on his land without permission, in addition to shooting his birds.

We didn't have much of an answer. We collared our dogs, promised we wouldn't return, crossed our fingers, our eyes, our bootstraps, yodeled quietly as if awaiting a whipping, and then we snuck back the next week.

As a ranch hand on another property years later, it was my assignment to kick hunters off the land, and I wasn't much good at it.

They weren't a whole lot different than Honer and me at sixteen, and the land was broad.

"You're on private property, you know."

"We just tracked a wounded doe across."

"That your tree stand?"

"Well, ... Uh-huh."

"Probably should take it down when you go."

The Idaho legislature recently adopted a bunch of new trespassing rules that have given hunters in a state where hunting on another's property was sort of a right of passage — it being neighborly and everyone knew it — a queer jolt.

Before the latest rule change, most private lands were haphazardly posted if at all. Fences, if they existed, were dictated by livestock and therefore necessary unless the cows lumbered on rangeland not bounded by barbed wire.

Most landowners took the same tack as me when confronting a hunter on land where they paid the taxes. They might ask for the courtesy of a call next time, and then help drag out your buck.

It's that bone stuck in your craw, somewhere near the bottom of your tongue, next to the gag reflex, to know that the men and women you elected, have now elected to saddle you — meaning us Idahoans — with an odious law that I'm told, allows landowners to shoot trespassers if they deem them an irrational intrusion.

I spoke with a fellow hunter I met the other day at a gated entrance to state land. He assured me it was our representative's chumminess with attorneys representing gigantic out-of-state interests that led to the latest trespass laws. He called it a new land ethic crafted by monied outsiders who want to bust up the union of neighborliness that Idahoans have lived with for the better part of a century.

For the many landless hunters out there, however, take heart and recall that North Idaho, in addition to its liberal chunks of endowment lands, boasts more federal acres open to hunters than we deserve.

Almost three million? Say, what?

A recent pact between the fish and game department and the state lands bureau puts more than two million additional acres of Idaho endowment ground in our back pocket, in case the rest is full.

There is enough of this public land that we hunters can hump for days while running dogs, chasing birds, elk, and deer without confrontation.

And we need not ask for permission.

That is a good thing for Idaho and has more to do with the foresight of the fish and game department and the ties of many of its employees to the land they grew up on than to legislators we elected to protect our interests. More and more of them are propped by the corporate or political bullies of other Western states who feel the need to change our landscape into the kind that has been indelibly squandered elsewhere.

The remedy is to stay diligent. Given that voting records and legislation are easily accessed, even on a cell phone, there is no excuse for being ill-informed.

The terrain is changing and it doesn't take a satellite map to see it.

Fall is the season for chasing game and for making change. The blunderbuss is used for one while the ballot box is for the latter.

It's good to live in a land that affords us the opportunity to do both.

Last Season's Hunts

Messed up, he said. Screwed the pooch.

"I had two good bucks pass by my stand in an hour and I didn't shoot either one," the man said before asking me about my latest season hunting North Idaho whitetails.

We sat on plastic five-gallon buckets turned upside down and stared into small holes bored in the ice watching our bobbers.

In states known for big game, ice fishing is often used to recount the glory days of September, October and November when we were hunters, once, and younger.

We do this while sitting silently, sometimes stomping our feet to entice heat into our extremities while watching a bobber float on the frigid black water of a small, chiseled hole long after the deer season is over.

Ice fishing is a time to deeply reminisce.

A friend of mine sent a voice message that I saved from a September day when he muddled a shot on a bull elk, thereby permanently besmirching his image as The Guy Who Doesn't Miss.

"That was the first elk I missed since high school," he said under his breath before returning to the real estate office where he quietly sits most days seeking property for people from coast to coast. He discreetly taps laptop keys, hushes and shushes, and feels lonely as a long-haired goat in a suburban backyard for screwing up that shot.

The year my pal missed the bull, and the guy let the bucks pass anticipating a bigger buck would come along, a guy named Russell had a perpetual grin that would snuff the scowls of the most melancholy ice fishermen.

I know this because I met Russell at a gas station at four in the morning on the day before Thanksgiving. A skiff of snow covered streets and yards, but snowfall in Russell's yard in the northwest corner of the Panhandle known as the snow belt, was already heavy and deep. I was fueling my beat up all-wheel drive economy wagon to make sure I had the juice for the trip to my deer stand when I noticed this guy standing beside an old pickup truck with a grin that couldn't be attributed to the freshness of the gas station sticky buns.

I had to ask.

Russell was keen to explain his cheerfulness.

He had a day ago killed a massive buck near Priest Lake and was unabashed about sharing the story with pretty much anyone regardless of their disposition or propensity for envy.

He thrust a photograph of a massive whitetail buck into my field of view as the gasoline pump clicked, stopping on a total of $53 to fill the tank of a Subaru.

Those were economically woeful times and hunting seemed the panacea for the drought of jocularity.

Russ was its testament as he stood under the sallow lights of the gas station grinning ridiculously holding a snapshot of a buck that lay dead in deep snow near a patch of brush. The deer was a relic, its antlers were giant claws of nut-colored bone, its hair a thick ruff to stave off the high mountain cold. Its tongue was out on one side, almost like a middle finger and with the rut over, the deer's last days after having passed its genes to numerous does, seemed an aggravation. It appeared happy to finally be dead.

Russ relayed his tale with some gusto and just enough humility to keep it interesting. The Old Town, Idaho, logger and some pals were driving to a job site when they saw a deer cross the backroad. Russell's pantry at the time was more or less meatless except for a can of Dinty Moore beef stew, so he bailed from the vehicle and tracked the deer through the falling snow catching up as it stopped in a cluster of trees. It showed a shoulder and rump, both of which looked like they would make a fine roast.

Drooling slightly with anticipation, Russell shot the deer for meat, he said and was rewarded with a lot more.

He pushed piles of white stuff ahead of him as he trudged, thigh deep to where the deer lay.

"I saw the antlers sticking up," he said.

Then he beamed like a pair of blue halogens.

The whitetail Russ shot had a jungle gym on its head and sported forked brow tines. It was bigger than a beast he had killed years earlier, which vied for the record books, Russell gushed.

The deer in the photograph under the gas station lights would cast him forever as a hunter of a different fraternity.

He didn't say this. He didn't need to.

If Russell ice fishes — I'm not sure he does — the memory of that buck will warm him like eiderdown when, in another perhaps fruitless season, he's sitting on a bucket on the ice sipping tag soup. Because underneath the Stormy Kromer flap-eared cap and Johnson Woolen Mills bibs and the Baffin pac boots, and removed from the huffing into fists to keep his hands warm, Russell will forever belong to the bevy of North Idaho wall-hanging hunters who are easily distinguished by their smirks. Eternally set apart from the school of deer chasers who need no practice missing, or second-guessing, or otherwise muffing a shot Russell will be warmed by the glow of his dead eye and decisive action.

Hunters who sat on cold, plastic, five-gallon buckets that year staring ruefully into the maw of black water through holes in the ice would have been warmed by the alpenglow Russ exuded.

"That buck is going to score in the upper 70s or 80s by looking at it," he grinned under the gas station lights as he measured the deer's antlers in his mind.

It was a grand whitetail by any standard.

"It could be in the running for the state record book," he mused.

Record book or no, it was a fine deer, and it certainly made stew.

And probably jerky.

Which, spooned from a hot thermos, is wonderful to have along on an ice fishing trip.

An Autumn Hunt With A Dog And A Gun

We smelled them before we saw them, the dog and I.

We were back at the old homestead and the forester said his company had once again logged that valley where years earlier I had chased an elk, spooked it with too much bugle and it skulked away, but not without letting me know its surrender was reluctant.

Next time, it seemed to say. Next time, let's do this.

The sun was getting high that day and the steam from the fallen tree trunks met the warming autumn air as I picked my way across the down cedar at the edge of the clearcut.

The sharp limbs snapped and cracked like cold cereal under my soles as I blew on the elk bugle, squealed, and mewed pleadingly for that bull to come back.

He had left for good, though, trotted into the swamp and likely over the ridge onto another less crowded, north-facing slope.

Today, however, the dog and I slipped into the lowlands

below the new cut, where the loggers left a strip of timber along the creek thick with alder.

We had agreed that morning, the dog and I, to walk and hunt what we called the loop, a grouse hunter's path that kept to the aspen sidehills, the clumps of snowberry bushes and elder patches. It wound in and out of early sun, before dropping to the creek bottom. From there it climbed into the real thick stuff, vine maple and dogwood that prevented a hunter from swinging a gun, before the path broke out, crossing chunks of wet meadow stippled with cedar.

The loop was a few miles of North Idaho backlands that edged dirt roads and side stepped locked gates that the forester said, "go on through."

As long as you're walking, the company doesn't mind, he said. It's ATVs that aren't welcome.

So we bypassed the green company gates too, walking the rights of way, and ended in the bottomland along the new clear cut at the exact location where, during cool autumn mornings with another dog — gone now — I had been greeted by the thunder of ruffed grouse blowing from the berry patches. The birds tumbled into the dark crevasses of cedar where BBs from a shotgun blast couldn't reach them.

A big culvert here let the stream flow downhill. In spring, cutthroat trout, fat as a forearm and red-sided, finned to the flooded swamp to spawn before heading back to the river.

This morning no grouse was there, but the smell of elk wafted through the place like a barnyard and we stopped to take it in.

The dog's tail wagged, he knew something special was about to happen. His nose stabbed the air.

I held the over-under shotgun in one hand and clicked the safety since there were no birds to swing at, and inhaled what I knew to be the perfume of distant elk. Not Herefords. Not out here.

The fences that kept cows in had long fallen down. Their posts were bleached and green-mossed. Their barbed wire rusted and buried in duff.

The people who ran the cattle and mended the fence, who had charcoaled the split cedar posts to keep them from rotting too quickly, had quit, moved on, or died.

The place, once part of a larger ranch that kept a section all to itself, was now eyed by investors and real estate agents.

Cattle were no longer a necessary commodity.

But the timber companies were slowly making a much-needed comeback, and the latest clearcut would in time provide food for deer, elk and grouse.

We trailed slowly through the meadowrue, camas and clover of the dew-dampened low ground. The morning had been spectacular. Not another person had we met, nor had we grimaced at the revving of an approaching ATV. There was none. The land, that day, despite a few new houses in places where we once waited patiently for dusk and the deer it released, was mostly the same as it had been a couple of decades earlier.

Even the long silence hadn't changed a lot.

For this we were grateful.

When the road switched back through the bottomlands we eyed the swales and edges of the clearcut and felt the morning breeze switch and blow across the hill.

Then, just below a ridge near the tree line, the yellow rumps appeared almost pumpkin-like.

Then, more.

The cow elk picked their way through the down cedar, the dry bones of branches and brittle cartilage of cut trees.

They moved without a sound and appeared not to notice us.

Likely a bull drifted nearby. Experience said so. Likely it watched from timber's edge, waiting for the slow flux of our limbs because any movement meant danger. But we were transfixed. The dog stopped his wagging. The aroma that curled down from the herd was intoxicating.

It said you've been gone too long from this dirty, sweating, hands-on-knees sneaking, cow calling, cartridge chambering, glassing and air gulping, sweet science of elk hunting.

C'mon, it said. You remember.

As our ears synced with our eyes in that October light we heard them talk. It was a distant mewing sound like cats.

Elk talk. An ancient exuberance.

We listened and relished the fragrance as if it were new.

And then slowly, with the breeze, we slipped unobtrusively back down a grassy, overgrown road and through cedar shadows.

The dog wagged, and the elk ebbed away too.

What We Know About Elk And Snowy, Late-Season Hunts

It started to snow and didn't quit.

The flakes were big and slow, covering the sky and providing a kind of screen for the elk that moved out of the canyon and through the open glades of yellow pine to the plateau.

When the elk reached the hay fields, they were single file, a slow procession that kept mostly to the swales. They topped off on the lee side of a knoll heading for the timber that sprouted like a high and tight haircut on the other side of the cut fields.

Their destination was a deep grove of fir, cedar, some spruce. The well-covered benches held browse, blocked the wind, and in general provided a good place to hole up.

From a mile away, looking north across the canyon from a hogsback ridge — there are houses now — you could see them.

"The herd always does that," a man who lived near the ridge told me.

When it snowed, he would wobble in a pickup truck along a two-track — the road is paved now — to the high ground and watch them.

"The first big snow pushes the herd out of the canyon and in a single file across the plateau to the timber," he said. "It's the same most years. Thirty head, maybe more. A few raghorns and spikes the rest are cows."

From the ridge their rumps, wapiti, visible as a hunter's cap.

I hunted grouse at the edge of the timber when the snow started to fall and didn't let up. I had forgotten what the man had told me years earlier about the elk in that canyon. I sat on a stump at the edge of the forest and waited for the snow to let up. It covered my tracks. Suddenly I saw elk heads bob over a swale, saw the dark and light-colored capes, the ruff, and ears press forward. Seemingly from nowhere, as the man said, the elk in single file moved slowly through the falling snow across the high plateau and made a beeline in my direction.

The snow was silent. It covered sound. Sometimes a breeze huffed in my face or blew crossways. Errant gusts skirted a shoulder or occasionally crawled down the back of my neck. One of those stopped the elk.

The lead cow, ambling until then, raised suddenly up. She rigidly lifted her head and stopped. Smelling the breeze she barked to alert the others. Still as stacked cordwood, their eyes pierced like arrows through the falling snow and into the patch of crabapples trees where I now crouched with my bird gun on my lap and binoculars raised.

I was less than a quarter mile away at the edge of the timber they expected to reach without fuss.

They had, however, found fuss.

It was me.

I crept back into the fanning arms of young fir and circled around and away in an effort to not interrupt their migration. By then, however, the herd had broken rank and spread west over snow-covered furrows where it likely regrouped, maybe forming another less rigid file that slipped more quickly down the timbered slope on my flank.

This is one thing we know about elk.

When I moved out to a house in the hollers, tight lips were the rule.

Not many people spoke about elk. A man who lived a long time up the road said there was no elk hunting season when he built his farm in the gulch around the time the big deer were introduced into the country more than a half-century ago.

Without hunting, the elk herds grew.

Eventually, the farmer, unsuccessful at keeping the big deer from his crops, complained to the game warden. The ungulates busted his fences and bored winter hay piles meant for his cows and horses.

The warden, a taciturn man, gaunt and smoking a pipe came out a few times to inspect the damage.

One day, he turned to the farmer and said, "It looks like you'll need to develop a taste for elk meat."

The farmer eventually hung a heavy set of antlers on his barn, and when a hunting season opened he supplemented his income with guided horseback packs into the hills.

Lanterns, canvas tents, bedrolls, and rifles.

The people who moved into the valley much later needed their own freezers filled. They changed the topic when elk were mentioned.

Clues to the elk's existence were there if you looked:

See the broken dogwood, its limbs chewed.

Elderberry bushes trampled.

A shed antler found in a draw, sun-bleached on one side, brown on the other.

Just one.

A track.

On a hillside, at first light, a cow picked her way through a brush field talking quietly to a calf.

"The elk have always been in there, ever since I can remember," said a man who grew up in the holler and now sells tires in town. "Not a lot of folks know it."

The landscape changes. Driveways, private gates, "No Trespassing" markers, fences, and neighbors you never see except in a pickup truck when their haste runs you off the dirt road. You once killed a buck in their yard when it was only trees and deer trails. That's where a shop and house with a vaulted ceiling now sit.

But when the snow falls the secretive herd of elk files from the canyons into the quiet, covered benches where you can catch them. Because that is what they do this time of year.

It's one thing we know about elk.

When the regular hunting season is over and rifle hunters are home watching football games on TV, and the snow comes down fat and makes the forest silent, you might walk right up on a small herd in the forested glades on the high side of the plateau. The animals, their capes catching snow, will look quizzically through you.

It is the season for mittens and front-loader rifles that shoot just one ball at a time. You are acutely aware of your breathing, how its heat turns to cold fog. You hear your footfalls and see paw prints in the tracking snow.

That is what we know about December elk hunters.

It's Magic Out There, Bring Some Warm Socks

The shivers take a toll.

Teeth chattering, and sometimes heart-thumping, can throw a hunter off his or her game which usually includes making a clean shot for a quick kill, but may also entail the simple art of concealment.

Say for instance a bunch of cow elk stroll past and a bull brings up the caboose.

Cows, just as does — be it mulies or whitetails in this part of the sphere — are keen observers of their surroundings because staying upright is their business and keeping the next generation alive is paramount.

So, they live, to borrow a phrase, with their heads on a swivel.

While you're poised in the shadows with your bow fully drawn, a cow will notice if you frown a fly off your forehead or scrunch tight your eyes to shoo away a glossy aphid that invaded a tear duct. Or, maybe it wasn't the facial movement, but the errant whisper of a breeze that for a fraction of a second touched the back of your ear and lifted the head of the browsing cows in unison, like a water aerobics team. Their eyes locked on yours. Their stereo smell and three hundred fifty million receptors channeled a bark.

Now what?

Once as a teenager in a tree stand, after having derided the concerns of some pals who embraced a phenomenon they called buck fever, I heard my heart jump in my chest as a four-by-four buck walked through the frozen swamp below me.

I packed a .32 Special lever action rifle with a three-power scope. It was a brush gun that belonged to my dad who had graduated to more refined hardware.

The whitetailed buck was in sort of a hurry. It walked the same path where minutes before I had watched an ermine hunt voles. I had the rifle poised at the footfalls of the deer coming, the rustle of dried leaves and occasional twig snap as my breath frosted my face but it was my loudly-banging heart that stopped the buck in his tracks.

Buck fever, I heard myself whisper.

A man in Clarkia once told of tracking elk through fresh snow to the top of a plateau, stepping in their tracks, and when he reached the summit the elk had disappeared. Their tracks didn't betray their direction they just ended, the man said. It was as if the elk had taken flight.

He backtracked, then ringed the mountain top until he once again picked up the tracks. This time heading down.

The animals, when they had reached the peak aware of a

pursuer, lept forty yards over the edge without leaving a trace, he surmised.

All without a sound.

I chuckled at the tale until years later, arriving in a honey hole after a long trek through sleet in the dark, I was met with elk talk. There were mews, squeals, and a bugle. A group was mucking it up nearby. I crouched under the low black limbs of a fir for an hour until shafts of morning sun pressed in and I couldn't stay still.

Freezing temperatures, the lack of movement, and the sweat I had built on the hike made a ragdoll of me. My teeth chattered. My body was an electric sander turned on high.

Seemingly from nowhere, a bull appeared to fence with a small tree a stone's throw before me. A halo of sun surrounded him. The light danced on his antlers like an angel abra carousel.

I mustered the energy to keep from vibrating like a tuning fork and slithered a few yards to a down log to rest the rifle and keep from messing a shot.

Face down and squeezing my eyes shut, I slid the rifle gently over the log and counted. On the count of five, I would hold my breath and compress my shivering body into a stoic and muscle-still killing machine.

With my body transformed in that disciplined moment of non-movement, I raised my head and peered through the scope to an empty spot where the bull had been.

No sound had ushered his retreat.

The small fir remained, bark peeled. Newly stripped limbs

hung broken in the soft stream of sun.

The herd was gone too.

I stood up, and like an exorcism allowed my entire body to shiver and shake and my teeth to loudly chatter.

With the ruckus diminished, I walked through the woods to where the group of elk had been.

Nothing.

Just their scent. Not even a print. In a freshet that always ran clear, I found swirls of muddied water.

The man from Clarkia had a point.

It's magic out there. Embrace it. And carry an extra pair of dry mittens and socks.

Gold In Them Hills

To learn the agitated art of gold panning we went north, but we needn't have gone so far.

It was common for people camping up north to have a gold pan in their backpacks along with a floppy hat. The two went hand in hand. Whiskers completed the package that called for denim pants and rolled-up sleeves, a trowel, perhaps, maybe the kind of smokeless tobacco that left a ring in a shirt pocket.

Nupic and Faye were gone two weeks looking for gold and came back heavily laden with gear, a rubber raft, sluice boxes, pumps and pans, and a few vials of the powdery kind of precious metal called dust in the movies. They had some nuggets too, the size of bead head nymphs and if their find did not pay the cost of the trip, it imbued them with a certain fever that kept charts and topographic maps unrolled on their kitchen tables as they traveled, panned, sluiced and dredged aloud in their kitchens until the next expedition.

In the winter, home-made schnapps fermented in a ceramic pot on top of Nupic's refrigerator. It sometimes dribbled from cups or was splashed on the maps dousing the ash from burned tobacco that left small holes like flyspecks.

Plans seemed exceedingly urgent and animated.

A man in St. Maries told of gold claims on Soldier Creek where the old road climbed the hill then dropped into Santa along the St. Maries River.

He remembered the men who worked the claims from his boyhood, but he was in his 80s when he died a decade ago.

Once in Nome, a kid who was much younger than me showed me how to pan for the glittery stuff after he spent months developing, then satiating an appetite for finding gold.

He owned a pump and stainless steel sluice box, but the pump's impeller kept clogging, so he regularly turned to the pan. Either way, he pointed out gold particles in the mesh of his sluice or in the rusty pores of his metal pans. He plucked at them with a fingernail before sucking the particles up with a snuffer or picking them from the mesh with a tweezer.

I expected something meatier, more golf-ball-like. Something that could weigh down a pant pocket, but we didn't find that.

On our way to get rich real fast, Boggsy and I found a shaft that went straight back into a hill.

We learned of the abandoned claim from an old document at the county courthouse along with many other forgotten claims left to Mother Nature's endless mitigation.

The shaft was big enough for two people to stand up in, side by side if they didn't mind being close with their necks kinked. Stalactites like the bottoms of new carrots dripped from the carved rock overhead as we worked our way carefully to the end with a flashlight. It was winter. The sky outside was gray and the world was wet.

We didn't spot gold veins or seams and likely whoever cut the tunnel just gave up.

Gold is where you find it someone will say. It's not where it isn't. That kind of erudition pays for itself.

Skill considers synclines and anticlines, outcrops, and the indicators that narrow the odds and lead to the place on the map where the witching stick of preparation hastens the likelihood of a find.

Finding even gold flakes often requires more than luck or magic, though, but either will work in a pinch.

Last week my son and I stuck a couple of metal pans into a stream we know.

We dug the muck and dirt from a flume of submerged gravel in a bend where heavy rock, carried by spring runoff, would drop from the current.

We swished and swirled and picked through gravel, added water, and then did it again.

An afternoon passed. It was a moderate winter's day.

The only sound was the stream. Now and again the shadow of a bird crossed the ground.

The sun was warm in a blue and timeless sky.

We didn't find gold. Not a speck that we could tell.

Being out there with shovels and pans, a smiling dog, and

one's thoughts on a stream in the woods was its own soft and lustrous metal.

It was hard work, harder than I remembered from the days accompanying Nupic and Faye, and no fever struck.

Instead, we hiked out of the ravine with our pans and shovels and floppy hats and turned up the heater inside the pickup truck as we wearily headed toward home.

Drawing On Memory

My bow has wheels and the arrows have three razors.

The points I use on targets look like tiny Kyrgyz hats made of hardened steel. They drive into blocks of foam so deep it takes two hands and elbow grease to pull them out.

I know just as much about archery today as I did twenty years ago when the guy in the store in a small town with a fiberglass elk overlooking the main street said walk this way.

I had been perusing cheap ammo, running my fingers over topwater lures and ceramic tableware with duck motifs, burning time because back then time was plentiful as tinder.

"Put your hand right here, inside this braided leather loop," he said, thrusting an archer's bow in my direction. "Use this gizmo to pull the string."

I instinctively followed his instructions because nearly every month for several years a portion of my paycheck was entrusted to this shop owner and he regularly steered me away from poor purchases with four words.

"You don't want that," he would say, adding something about out of towners who took to shiny things like camp jays, and who possessed the pecuniary pluck to follow through.

"This one's for you," he would declare as if he could smell the sweat on the remaining bills in my pocket.

When I peered through the bow's peep sight as big as a puka shell my arrow pointed at a block of foam against a wall in the back of his store. In winter he hung ice augers and Christmas ornaments there.

"Touch that trigger," he said, and the floor creaked.

The string twanged softly and the arrow tarried forth like the tongue of a snake after a cricket. It plugged the target where I had pasted my eye, or pretty near that place.

"Waddya think?" He asked.

"Huh," I ventured with the academic acuity I considered as my stock and trade.

"Pretty nice," I added.

"Try it again," the man said, hooking his thumbs through the belt loops of his blue jeans as if he was planning to stay awhile.

"Two minutes and you can shoot that bow better'n you shoot your pistol," he stated. "Trust me."

He was right.

This man had owned the shop on the main drag of that town since someone decided that time could be measured by the age of a raccoon, and he once took me outside on a cool autumn morning when traffic was sparse to nonexistent and pointed to a hill. Years earlier, he whistled a bull elk to his bow up there using a cartridge casing.

Back then, the man said, there was an elk behind every tree.

"It was like calling your dog," he said. "You know what I'm saying?"

I sent another arrow across the floor of the back room, zipping past a neoprene wader display, sacks of goose decoys, and boxes of inflatable boats that could be carried with some effort to mountain lakes and used to fish hard-to-reach places.

The thud meant the arrow found that red spot in the middle of the target he called sweet.

"That arrow will go right through an elk," the man said.

He grinned and nodded his head like he was watching someone shoot a bow for the first time.

"Nock another one!"

I spent the better part of the afternoon wearing khakis and a button-front shirt sending colorful sticks with plastic feathers into a wall of foam inside the local sporting goods store when I should have been across the street in an office dripping coffee on my shoes.

After signing up for six easy payments, I walked out of the place carrying a camo-colored bow made of aluminum alloy that cost less than a set of snow tires. It had fiberglass limbs with two wheels called cams, a side-mounted quiver, and a half dozen, made-to-fit arrows with plastic fletching that may be called vanes.

What I carried was more than a feat of engineering made in a secret enclave in Lewiston, Idaho, that bore an uneasy name,

Sidewinder. I knew I carried the key to a future of running shoe hunts in September in the high hills, ridge-straddling after elk talk — the mews, grunts, chuckles, and bugles. The future meant hours of horn watching and delicious frustration, exertion, and road maps made on napkins in cafes and parking lots in the best part of the state — its small towns. That's where you can tell an elk hunter by the smidge of face paint left on the corner of an eyelid, his or her dusty pickup truck, referred to colloquially as a "rig," and the choice of cologne.

"Psst ... Is that Golden Estrus I whiff, or Bull Fire?"

"Shhh. I call it waller juice. It's a special blend."

"Got any to spare?"

When late summer turns golden, and the nights are still warm, and lumpy camper trailers start taking root along mountainous two tracks, it's best to sneak by them really early. Slip into the hills before the log-loading machines fire up their engines and block the high roads with cut trees sorted to fit bunks of trucks that haul the wood to the mills.

Roll quietly past the hinterland hunting camps and then amble on foot sideways up a steep hill through the charcoal night, aiming your body directly at the constellation of the bear, eagle, or swan.

The stars cover the sky like sugar spilled on a tabletop. The night hike is honeyed and sweet as a thump-ripe melon.

Before the first slick of day makes shadows you'll be among elk and their soliloquies will be yours to pluck.

All you need to know about a bow is that it's light and fast, its arrows have three razors that drive silently and efficiently through animals big as a steer.

Gizmos, such as egg-shaped cams and silencers, shock absorbers, and magnifiers may be new, but archery hasn't changed a lot.

It's about being where you want and putting an arrow where you want it.

It is about ridges and trails, quiet places that turn thunderous faster than a summer squall, and just as quickly fall eerily silent, as if all that commotion, snorting, red-eyed glaring, and yodeling was dreamed.

It doesn't even matter if you send an arrow out, because humping the hills with a bow and rucksack feeds memory, and provides a lot of enchantment to draw from.

SOMEWHERE, IDAHO

The Roberts Gun

I bought the gun years ago while working at a cement plant during the day, and reading books that told how to reload brass cases at night.

I became acquainted with something called a wildcat round and was intrigued because it had a ring to it.

It sounded like something that may be light and quick and would, in times of trouble, land on its feet.

I sought out a caliber that would shoot flat, with a peppy bullet that could knock down a coyote from a fair distance and an elk close up.

What I found at first — after many pages turned by the light of a low-wattage bulb, accompanied by eyelids shutting and opening heavy as piano lids — was a name.

Like wildcat, Ned Roberts had a good sound and there was a time when the man himself carried with him a stellar reputation as a ballistician, firearms experimenter, a developer of wildcat cartridges, a marksman, and gun writer.

A picture of a lean Ned Roberts, baggy-eyed under a brimmed hat with a mustache like Rudyard Kipling, shows him seated in what appeared to be a New England backyard in the early 1900s. He holds a slender rifle with a long, spyglass scope. The black and white picture drips nostalgia and the grit in Roberts' eye had me kicking down to the local hardware store to idle over its rifles and accouterments.

Maj. Ned Roberts and some pals had for many years appraised .25-caliber single-shot rifles, and the retired major had designed the .257 Roberts, named for him, as a compromise between a flat-shooting, low recoil, varmint caliber, and the bigger 30-calibers made for large game.

The cartridge attributed to Roberts was developed in the 1920s and marketed a decade later. For a time, it was one of the most popular calibers around, a favorite for shooting pronghorns across big pieces of Montana and Wyoming, elk and deer in sloping Rocky Mountain cover, and coyotes over farm fields.

The hardware store clerk could pretty much order anything, he said, but on the shelf was one particular gun with a hand-checkered walnut stock that, along with an American-made 3 x 9 power scope, would cost me an entire paycheck.

"I'll take it," I said.

The following week, I turned over my payday to the clerk and carried the Roberts rifle home.

The firearm, a Ruger Model 77 in .257 Roberts was the first rifle I purchased after inheriting a cabinet full of others.

After 30 years it remains a favorite because like a lot

of things, rifles start with a history lesson. As time goes on, around them smolder stories of friends and campfires, rucksacks and climbs, ungulates, some with antlers or horns, and some without, often in places too far away to mention, hunts and scenery and what may pass as adventure.

The sling from my .257 was once removed and used as a safety rope to lower myself from the side of a cliff I had scaled on a mountain goat hunt. The gun itself became a staff. Its barrel is speckled from sea salt, the result of bear and deer hunts on the coast and something I have been remiss to atone. The finish on the rifle's stock is flaked from being bumped and rubbed, and the stock itself has been tested against boat hulls, boulders, the beds of pickup trucks.

My pal Boggsy refers to the gun as a "2-5-7 Robbie," and sometimes I do as well. We've been a lot of places together, this rifle and me, so a familiar moniker seems apropos.

Winter, we know, is a fine time to get reacquainted.

Maybe we'll drive to the range for a boisterous and hopefully accurate conversation on paper.

It's always a good idea.

Just me, the radio and my 2-5-7 Robbie.

Winter

Arizona On My Mind

A friend of mine called me from Arizona.

Rattlesnakes, he said.

Lots of them.

He was standing in the middle of a field, he said, on a chair.

They are freaking me out, he said.

A neighbor in the camping spot where my friend stays during winters away from his Priest Lake home shot two of them with a .22 pistol, he said.

They were harassing his dogs or vice versa.

One of the snakes had a rattler with 10 buttons. It stood up like a banjo showing its tongue.

Those things are crafty, he said, they hide in the woodpile, under the drain tile, they are in the wheel wells and outhouse and he thinks they are balled up in a gopher hole behind the fire pit.

There are more snakes this winter than in time's past, he said, and they are devious without trying, tough and old, and will hit you like a hammer, sometimes twice and from there, it's months of recovery if your luck holds out. And they smell, he said. It's not a good smell, like elk, pine duff, or even the scratch pile of a mountain cat.

Then he asked why I had not caught a whitefish.

This is the same pal I once met years ago on the rim of a holler a few miles from blacktop as I took a breather in a place where one particular bull elk weeks earlier had marked a cobble of trees with his antlers. It was not an uncommon spot to catch a whitetail — one of the big ones — sneaking past, keeping to the shadows.

His dress was old-fashioned, wearing wool and flannel. He moved fast using his scope for binoculars like we all did back then and I yelled to make sure he knew I wasn't fair game.

I learned he had logged, hunted, and fished through most of the backcountry, a lot more than me, and with success. If years later I ever had a question about a hunting or fishing locale, he set me straight.

Once on Jungle Creek, he said, the elk bugled all night as he attempted to sleep to rise early to fell trees for the logging nearby. He stumbled from his camp trailer chasing off the nuisance bulls by clanging pots and pans.

When my car broke down on the way to hunt elk early one morning near a major road 12 miles from Coeur d'Alene, I heard a bull bugle and gave chase. There was no cell reception, but I had my bow.

I trespassed on the ground that years earlier had no warning signs and despite coming within feet of the bull I didn't let fly an arrow. Too much brush.

You might have gone around the backside of that hill, my friend told me. He had killed a few bulls on the lee side away from the road a decade ago, or more.

I once talked to a man who spends his free time fishing. He knew my pal.

He's a killer, he said.

They had hunted together and spotted a big buck on the other side of a swamp like a moat that was rimmed with ice.

My pal stripped down to his underwear, traversed the pond, shot the deer, and floated it back. They dressed and dragged the buck to the pickup truck.

Absolutely, this man said.

When I spotted a large bull elk at the edge of a meadow not far from town surrounded by homes that were outside the price range of most of us, I called my pal to tell him what I'd seen.

"We used to hunt the heck out of that when we were kids," he said.

He and his buddies, laden with firearms, rode bicycles there and then called their parents when they filled a tag.

He used a knife his dad gave him to field dress elk.

He still has the knife.

And once years ago, I asked if he had been up Ramsey Road, by the cemetery.

Houses, I said. Lots of them

He hadn't been there in a decade or more but had hunted the hayfields for whitetails back in the day.

This was the man who was standing on a chair in a field in Arizona because of snakes.

I am just tired of the winters back home, he said. Just tired of the cold.

Then he asked again why I hadn't caught a whitefish.

No talent for it, I told him.

He extolled on the best place to catch winter whitefish on one particular North Idaho river.

He wasn't planning to return home any time soon, he said.

Too much snow, he replied and there was the matter of snakes.

"I can't leave this chair because of them. They are freaking me out."

Boots And Old Baggage

In winter, I preferred bunny boots.

They were made with great helpings of white felt, had canvas straps, brass buckles, and no tread so they were slippery on snow and ice, but their panache made up for the shortcoming.

And they were warm.

I received my first and only pair as a nine-year-old and walked to Russ Pascuzzi's 76 Station with a metal gasoline can for the Ski-Doo, which is pronounced skee-dew with an accent up front, like TV.

Gasoline, I think, cost a buck a gallon but I can't remember. I concentrated on the walk.

Bunny boots, at least mine, made a jingling sound that attracted dogs. Caused them to perk their heads up like grazing deer that whiffed gun oil.

Lacking the flee instinct of cud-chewing ungulates though, the schnauzers and mistreated spaniels, the occasional

Chesapeake Bay retriever with bad teeth, the bone chewing Rotts and shepherds sensed my vulnerability. Wearing red flannel or flash orange, because hunting season seemed always in the offing, I teetered gingerly down the icy street toward my neighborhood swinging a gallon can of gasoline that I perceived could be used as a weapon.

It sloshed a little and dripped as I leaned this way and that, careful not to reveal misgivings.

Dogs sense flunkies, I am told, like the guy who lives in a basement with empty boxes of pizza. Let them smell trepidation and you'll be scrambling haphazardly down the street in your bunny boots bumping into mailboxes, spilling mixed gas on the front of your pants, and generally trying to keep your balance as you try to stay ahead of the snarling mutts.

My pal, Honer, told me to bag the bunny boots.

"Forget 'em," he said. "I'll take my pac boots over 'dem bunnies any day. They look like powdered donuts."

I feared Honer was right.

After running through a neighbor's corral to cover my scent after a particularly obnoxious dachshund made tracks toward my jingling boots, the once ivory-colored felt took on a tawny cast.

Honer's pacs — Sorels — were made of rubber. They were quiet and had leather up top. Inside where it belonged was the felt.

They didn't slip too much on the ice.

Despite conceding the practicality of Sorels, for a couple

of winters, I walked with a certain whispery smugness past snoozing dogs to Russ Pascuzzi's gas station as duct tape silenced the buckles of my bunnies.

Then I outgrew them.

And I never found a pair to replace the tainted, jingly boots my mother donated to the church rummage sale.

It doesn't matter anymore.

Bunnies were a rare item even then. Nowadays, there might be a mismatched pair at Sal's Surplus behind the case of chunky bean and chicken MREs.

Honer, too, outgrew his Sorels.

His were the boots he slipped off one clear winter morning, slinging them over a shoulder by their laces as the moon hung like a frozen melon in a river oak.

He walked to his deer stand in his socks, carrying his pacs because the soles squeaked on the sub-zero snow and Honer had the savvy of a woodsman even in middle school.

He shot a nine-by-eight swamp buck that morning and the mounted deer head with thread on its lips graced the wall of his bedroom long after the Sorels were tossed out.

Those boots too are obsolete. The original manufacturer, Kaufman Rubber Company of Kitchman, Ontario, quit the business and sold its name.

None of this matters because winter boots are as ubiquitous as shower sandals these days. They come in a variety of colors and soles. Some jingle, some squeak, some emit atomized scents that attract rutting bucks, and others are self-cleaning like Whirlpool ovens.

If you asked Honer, though, he'd probably just as soon have his old Sorel pac boots back.

Sometimes I miss the bunnies if only for their zest, and an uncanny ability to summon canine company.

Whitefish Can Wait

The best time to catch whitefish on a fly rod is in July when you're fishing for trout.

Putting aside as malarkey the commonly clung to conviction that whitefish are a winter phenomenon will help you sleep better and save you a lot of money on hand warmers and thermal gear.

Standing outside when the snow dribbles and the river clinks with ice and your fishing rod guides are plugged like a toddler's nose at Petri Dish Daycare is what a friend refers to as punchy.

As in, "We must be pretty punchy to be out here doing this."

I hear his voice, but sometimes he's hard to locate through the sideways falling snow and wind on the river in February.

Jacques is a former boxer who pursued a career in the medical field and called me once from college in Michigan where he worked out on a heavy bag in a gym, while distancing himself from the ring, to say matter of factly, "If

I had known the brain damage caused by fighting, I would have done ballet."

He fishes too. Sometimes with me, and he is a student of natural history.

He likes whitefish because they are native to our western rivers and streams, and chasing them gives him something to do in winter, although we have lately concluded our tactics are off-kilter.

Hence, the fusty term, "punchy" for endeavors that are ill-advised.

Mountain whitefish are a native species with scales like quarters that flake off and glisten in the sun. Their smallish snout is perplexing and when they fight on the hook they throb, dive, and run like a schnauzer before giving up.

They are pulled in with anticipatory glee that invariably turns sourpuss when the angler, hoping for a fat, lazy trout sees a plump whitefish on the line, dour as a brush salesman at happy hour.

The fish is glum and resigned. It appears sad, and the angler's demeanor too is downcast.

In winter though, when you're fishing for whitefish because you still have not used the Little Chief smoker you received as a gift three Christmases ago, the native fish with their flaky smoked meat are a marvel.

And they are more difficult to catch in ice-banked rivers than in summer trout haunts.

One July evening on the Jefferson as the river surface stirred with hatching insects, we cast with joyous hearts

only to learn that mountain whitefish had invited themselves
to the bug-hatching food court. They voraciously snatched
fake flies as readily as rainbow trout, and more of the loutish
whitefish than rainbows were caught.

We threw them all back and concluded that despite its
standing as a winter sport, whitefish fishing is best reserved
for July or August.

Poised like a jitterbug on a snow-chunked riverbank in
February spooling line that has taken on the temperament of
licorice while you blow into a cold fist and pick the ice from
rod guides — all in an effort to introduce your smoker to a few
slabs of whitefish — is a healthier pastime than watching Dr.
Phil on daytime TV, but that's where its usefulness ends.

There are a lot of taverns near rivers where patrons
grumble about many things, but not whitefish fishing.
Inside, sports programs sputter on TV screens and music
plays. These places are dark when it's really bright outside.
Entrees include pickled eggs and breaded mozzarella sticks,
deep-fried.

Smoked whitefish isn't on any menu.

Winter anglers suppress knowledge of these comforts.

Instead, they cast yarn flies, soft hackles, or bead heads for
whitefish in the snow because this peculiar pastime evolved
in the days when the state fisheries department prohibited
winter trout angling in North Idaho rivers.

Angling for whitefish became a foil, and then it became a
thing.

The rules have changed. The rivers are wide open all year,

so whitefish need not be the sole target of a weighted caddisfly in winter.

Winter fishing like a pot roast remains a hearty endeavor, but no one will begrudge an angler for diverting his or her attention to a stool near a warm and spitting hearth in a tavern on the better side of cell phone reception.

Catching whitefish can wait, after all, until the deep afternoons in summer when it's barbecue not bar food that earns our appeal.

That Fly Fishing Guide School

I was down with it.

Let's go to Livingston and enroll in a fly fishing guide school, he said.

The idea started as many ideas back then in Butte, Montana, the home of the pasty, pork chop sandwich, and the original beer and chili breakfast.

The imagination and exuberance that come with knowing your town has an all-night chili place that also serves draft beer at 6 a.m. is infectious.

The magazine containing the article about the fly fishing guide school had been lying for weeks on the floor of a bathroom stall in a rental apartment down the hill from the Copper King's once opulent, but nowadays run-down palace. The apartment was a few blocks west of the street where the actor, producer, and screenwriter Sam Shepard filmed a most poignant scene that included a piano falling from a window.

An idea crafted in a quiet place, regardless of its value

as an epiphany, is exactly what Rodin had in mind when he blasted out a bronze, packed a cooler with ice, and headed out the door with a fly rod to cast for eel and carp in a tributary of the Seine.

Unlike our disheveled, unshaven lot, Rodin sported a proud coiffure and a fulsome and well-maintained man beard and he was ahead of his time.

We were a bit behind in ours.

The dog-eared magazine would, years later, pay me for rambling articles of fly rodding misadventures. That winter in Butte, however, the glossy magazine was barely familiar, partly because its cost was a deterrent.

This particular edition likely filched from a barbershop had corners bent, ads torn from its pages, and that one salient article. The exposé on the fly fishing guide school seemed to be favored by the stool sitters who courteously left the periodical for the rest of us.

I tore out the article, showed it to cohorts, and one of them, that night at a Main Street tavern, expounded in lively fashion on the virtues of bamboo and the responsibility of anglers to teach others the art of the fly.

Dammit.

Livingston at the time was known to me as the place where Dan Bailey had for more than a half-century developed and sold flies by mail order from his shop on Park Street. It was the fishing that brought the New York professor to the Montana cowtown during the war years and Bailey's shop — along with the bite — almost hooked my Uncle Jim, a journalist who ran a small newspaper of his own, into taking over a small but established broadsheet called the Livingston Enterprise.

These days the Enterprise is run by a friend of mine, an avid angler, in whose Butte apartment we first read of the town's fly fishing guide school, and who, when his generosity hatches, lets me stand knees locked in the bow of his dory as we careen in the current of the Yellowstone River hunting brown trout.

The fly fishing guide school that we attended was not in Livingston exactly.

Its post office box was in a building downtown and the men who ran the school traveled to a supermarket along the highway for supplies sometimes, but the school proper was an old converted ranch east of the prairie dog town. Below it, the river braided into walkable runs, and deer with velvet antlers, heavy already in June, fed on the lush hay grass and clover that rolled like fur on a hound's back.

We enrolled in the school and drove across the Continental Divide to meet the instructors whose names we recognized from the covers of books. It lasted a week the whole thing and is still remembered as one of those summer blessings you stumble upon a few times in your life. They can be counted on a hand or two.

Road trip cafes in small towns that serve a once-in-a-life triple burger that's mostly bacon with a side of pie, are among them. The artistry of a certain vista splashed by a setting sun. That, too.

Pottery shops on the beach of a prairie as broad as the sea. The smell of fresh-cut hay after driving all night.

Those belong to the blessings.

A friend in Idaho once had the run of several ranches decades ago that included trout-laden spring creeks. He speaks of those summer days with the reverence reserved for a Nirvana concert. The likelihood of re-living any of it, he understands, is preposterous.

That fly fishing guide school, however myopically stumbled upon, was a postmodern pastiche of casting, rowing, netting, playing chef and housemaid, beer runs and late-night philosophy around campfires whose sparks added to the brilliance of the Milky Way.

It was recognized, later, as a turning point.

We went our separate ways after that, all of us. Filling days with children and wives, mortgages and exes, new and better employment, and always old cars and pickups and the magnificence of a hundred landscapes mostly with a backdrop of mountains carved by rivers.

We learned that small adventures are opportunities acted upon, arising innocuously, sometimes in places unexpected.

And we learned what Rodin told us a century ago: When casting yourself nakedly on the precipice of what lies ahead, take your time, and enjoy the view.

Speed Slow, Memories Yes

Any memories? They asked. Any photos?

Negative on the photos, I said, but memories? Check.

Speed Seaford died at Harborview the other day.

They unplugged him.

Which, in a way, is apropos. He was never plugged in. Not really. Having spent the brunt of his living in logging camps on Prince of Wales Island where the CB radio ruled, even in the age of cell phones and high def.

Speed's definition of high was wrapped in elevation, and high definition meant the top line under a word in the dictionary.

He was hands-on, knew human nature and he talked slow. Therefore the nickname.

When they pulled the plug a month after he wrecked his four-stroke Norton motorcycle on a strip of highway heading from Thorne Bay to Klawock, his sons and daughters in law, his wife and many nephews, nieces and grandchildren asked if

I had any memories to share of Speed Seaford and I said, sure.

After these, there will be more, I said.

When you least expect it, they jump out.

It doesn't end.

I first met Speed in the Harbor Bar, an establishment with a view of a small piece of the shrimp and seine fleet between the shed walls of the canneries in Petersburg, Alaska, where herring once flashed for days as they boiled in the ocean with the sun on their scales and the salmon were so fat you could walk on their backs in the creeks they ran.

Those days were already a half-century gone when I met Speed at the round table by the only window in the place one sunny summer afternoon after spending the day in the woods slinging babbits. He nursed a bottle of Miller High Life beer and asked me, what do you do?

He's a choker setter, someone said, can't you tell by his fingernails?

Humpff, said Speed, through a gray handlebar mustache. He was never one to waste words.

Speed was well known by then as a top-notch construction boss and road builder and to join the crew of this man whose eyes were steely as his whiskers was to enter a fraternity of dawn to dusk workers and road-camp dwellers who were the best at whatever they did, with the bankroll to show it.

Two men talked loudly at the bar — long-winded fishermen from down south, Speed said. He wanted to fight them and asked what I thought of that.

I'm game, I replied, and he laughed like a walrus might and

hired me for a job that I still think of a lot.

Speed grew up in Libby, Montana, worked the roads and bridges from there to Bonners Ferry, married into a large family of railroaders, boxers, and baseball players, and took his bride north to a place called Coffman Cove at the edge of Clarence Straight where he put his education to work building roads.

Prince of Wales Island was considered the largest logging enterprise in the world and Coffman was a camp, a jumping-off and getting-on point where loggers in Filson tin pants, suspenders over striped rigging shirts, Romeo shoes and snuff cans stuffed into shirt pockets comprised the Sunday uniform. Any other day the Romeos were traded for caulk boots and metal hats replaced baseball caps.

The whole archipelago was a neighborhood and so I found Speed at the Harbor Bar 60 air miles north of Coffman. Or, maybe he found me.

I followed him to construction jobs in places like Nome and Trocadero Bay where, in winter, humpback whales breached in the waves ahead of the workboat with its windows frozen with spray.

Once, at a camp in Calder Bay, not far from the creek where logging-songster Buzz Martin was killed, Speed was in a backhoe churning up rock for a load as I and a fellow truck driver waited in the rain.

I stood by the cab with the Kenworth diesel chugging while Red sat on the ground behind his truck with a wrench trying to fix a brake.

Speed swung the working end of the backhoe around and called me over.

He leaned out of the cab as I scrambled up the rocks.

Tell Red, he said, that if he removes the top of that air can the spring will come loose and take his head clean off.

He powered up the machine and went back to work.

Red, the other driver, a novice who was turning the bolt that would release the can top, stopped when I said it. He filed the wrench in his pocket and retired to the cab of his truck.

I have friends I tell these stories to and they won't have it.

Once, in Alaska, they say and laugh because they have heard a few of them before.

They have their own lives and their own memory books.

If there is just one, however, that I am allowed to relay and take with, it's this.

In Nome where we hired on to build the Nome to Council highway cutting through tundra beyond the Safety Roadhouse of Iditarod fame, and over the Solomon River where on a knoll overlooking the Bering Sea the graves of Eskimos mix with miners and Chinese workers, a young Cat skinner once bellyached about the ineptitude of truck drivers.

We sat in the Polar Bar over beers and he aped on the ilk of the men behind the wheel of the big Terex trucks, their unsustainable density, and caustic stupidity.

Speed, his hand around a Miller High Life, looked at the man through steady eyes and with lips barely moving under the steel wool handlebar mustache responded quietly.

"Son, there is not a day on this earth when you can't learn

something from the lowliest truck driver."

I wanted for a while to tattoo that on my chest.

I didn't need to.

I keep it now with my memories of Speed.

The ones that come easy.

They all do, just at different times and some more frequently than others.

And when they emerge they are thick as honey or 90-weight transmission oil. They are viscous as his voice that flowed straight and thick like annealing.

Patiently, and just as slow.

In Spring, It's Snowshoes Or Skis

Spring in some places means the hellebore is in bloom.
In North Idaho, it means you can walk on snow.

It's a fickle business. We may not have the linguistic
dexterity often ascribed to the Inuit when it comes to cold
weather precipitation, but we know some things about the
white stuff.

In spring its crust can be hard as solid ground, so you either
walk on it or if the crust gets weak, punch a hole through it.
The former is better.

Postholing is the business of stepping on what appears to
be a sturdy piece of snow only to break through when pressing
your weight on the rind under your boot.

You punch a hole and sink in. And then you do it again, over
and over.

In our fair cities, many people in office shoes can be seen
postholing through spring snow on unshoveled city sidewalks
with the forlorn look of unfed owls. It's taxing and can turn a

docile office frog into a briefcase-chewing savage in less than the time it takes to posthole the length of a city block.

I knew a man who postholed through mountain snow uphill for a mile in spring to get a better look at what he thought was nearer his pickup. He had expected to walk on top of the snow to reach the scree field which led to the petroglyphs on the rock outcrops. But like the ancient drawings, distance and time took their toll and he spent the better part of the day slowly fading. He was exhausted and wet when he returned to the cab.

Postholing sucks your energy and lets snow into your boots unless you remember to wear gaiters.

The first proposition is dangerous, the latter annoying, while gaiters are just good sense.

Gaiters are tubes of waterproof fabric that cover the tops of boots to keep stuff, like snow and dirt, from falling in. They are a hallmark of cross country skiers who want to slide lightly on top of the snow, and snowshoers who shuffle, sometimes, through it.

To postholers, a myopic and enthusiastic bunch who might find part of an energy bar and an apple core from a previous misadventure at the bottom of their day pack, gaiters are an afterthought.

Posthole snow can be glided over on skis in spring when gale-force winds that turn North Idaho highways into snow-drifting catastrophes transform deep snow covering open fields into seamless solid surfaces.

Cross country skiers don't talk about it much, but

this phenomenon, when it occurs, is the making of home-spun adventure.

Getting blown across a mile of open field on skis in spring is relished by its practitioners with the indulgence reserved for similar outer-edge endeavors like bog snorkeling, chess boxing, or extreme ironing.

The concept was learned unintentionally by people gleeful to be blown away. They opened their coats to the wind and made a sail. The wind pushed them over fields and buried barbed wire fences as they shouted at each other like berserkers.

"Can you believe this? Wowowee!"

The same fields can be snowshoed, but more slowly.

Snowshoes are made for forests where the additional obstacles of brush and blowdown make skiing laborious.

The first snowshoes I strapped on under pac boots were bear paws, and we made trails through the swamp in the back of the house until May when the snow was a pitch of grainy diamonds before it disappeared.

The shoes were loaned by a neighbor and a few years later I owned a set of modified bear paws that were longer, with rawhide web and ash frames. Shuffling quietly through the woods in winter allows for animal watching and woodcraft. Native forest dwellers such as the Algonquins knew snowshoes were a survival tool that could result in fresh meat during the cold, snowy months instead of relying on a diet of pounded, dried pemmican. They could sneak up on game animals quietly and within range for a killing shot with an arrow or spear.

For postmodernists, there is a lot to see in the woods in winter without the pressure to see everything at once. But because March is the time of high mortality for our game herds, keeping one's distance is obligatory. The bulk of fawns and calves that become winterkill die in spring's deep crusted snow when their reserves are shot.

Postholing saps their energy and the forage found by pawing through snow isn't enough to keep up.

Animal watchers must keep their distance to prevent deer and elk from being pushed around the backcountry burning hard-won calories.

None of this should keep anyone from heading outside during the tawny days of spring to huff through the snow, or be blown over it.

Awareness is key. Grab the gaiters, and don't forget to pack a lunch.

Hard Water And Rooster Tails

George Lindley said it was like the time in Vietnam when he was caught with his pants down in a minefield.

Lindley was a tall man who after decades of slumping along with a fisheries biology degree was working on a master's. He was the student in the lab coat in a class of flannel shirts and T-shirts with nasty logos. He was the guy who was 20 years older than the rest of the class with his hair fading, and horn-rimmed glasses riding a bulbous nose.

As if to assure everyone that he was a little unclear about his station in life, he walked with a slouch that you could put a coffee cup on.

And his shoes were fourteen, double wide.

In Vietnam, he had been in the intelligence corps. He had studied dialects of the native language, but when he was called to duty he spoke mostly in the broken French he had learned in high school.

Out in the field somewhere south of the demilitarized

zone in a place where hot meals were served from packages of mostly powdered ingredients, and where living quarters were shared with rats big as barn cats, he and a few of his rank found a case of hootch. One night after a series of bluster and back-slapping that accompanied the swill of rotgut with the guys who carried the bandoliers, he found himself gurgling.

His gut rumbled, his head was a brass band and he felt a surge like two planets colliding somewhere in his solar plexus. A much-younger George then stretched his long legs and made marks in the clay dirt under a sickle moon with his big boots. He spent the next several hours producing strange noises with his backside until all sounds ceased, and something he referred to as "rice-water stools," stopped.

A slick of light from a rising sun marked his position.

He had left the wire of course in this backwood zone where nothing ever happened, but to his dismay, he realized that he had also left the path and had spent three hours crapping in a minefield.

As a man with a post-secondary degree — and he admitted, less sense than the guy humping a submachine gun through the muck — he casually zipped up.

Then George ran like hell.

He made it back inside the encampment without incident and told himself that next time if there was one, he would do what he learned in basics: He would stab the ground with his belt knife and carefully extract himself from the bouncing betties so as not to leave any of his body parts behind.

George told me this story one day in the aseptic offices of a university where he was a teaching assistant working on the advanced biology degree.

He told me this in light of a conversation about ice fishing.

He loved fishing of all kinds and never missed an opportunity.

So, one winter morning after three days of hard cold that George knew firmed up the new ice on a popular fishing spot not far from town, he set out.

He found the ice solid as he expected and clear as sake. It was at least four inches thick when he ventured out. The mercury clicked zero and the sound of his footfalls cracked on a skiff of old snow.

He was after spiny rays — perch, crappies, and the like — and had loaded his bucket with gear and dropped a few maggots in his lip like a dip of tobacco. Away he went.

Oh boy, out there on that lake he was slaying the buggers. Pulling fish from his slush hole and tossing them on the ice where they flipped and flopped before dying and freezing. Other anglers came out too and gathered around, drilling holes using swirly augers with Swedish names newly purchased at the local Big Box. Everyone was killing the pannies as the sun came up mellow and warm and George, the penultimate fisheries man, was catching like it was nobody's business.

Somewhere between his second and third sandwich and the last drop of cocoa from his thermos, with the sun glowering from high over the lakeshore pines and him in a T-shirt now, he heard a thump.

Water rushed to his feet.

Haha, he thought. What a superb day!

He looked around and realized he was the only person left on the ice.

He peered toward shore and saw a pickup, the last one in the parking lot aside from his beater Ford, totter up the road.

He heard ice cracking, a sort of boom, as ripples of water gurgled over the lake's surface toward him. Then the slick, wet platform underneath sort of slumped.

It had been at least 20 years since the minefield incident, but at that moment, like thick gravy slowly ambling over mashed potatoes on a potluck plate, it all came back.

George carefully raised himself from the plastic, five-gallon bucket where he sat. He gingerly reached for the now partially-frozen fish that floated in several inches of water. Plopping them carefully into his bucket and with the solemn consideration of a witness in a federal trial, he achingly reeled in his lines. When the poles had been placed into the bucket too, George remembered what he told himself those many years ago in that encampment not so far from the South China Sea as the sun rose and the moon slipped into a pink morning:

Keep calm. Use your head and your common sense.

Then, holding the bucket full of dead fish and gear in one hand and his empty thermos and auger in the other, he ran like hell.

As he relayed the tale I could see this man, who stood 6-4, dressed in heavy boots, with three layers of thermal gear wrapped around his waist like a tennis star, ungulate legs, shoulders perpetually slumped and the horn-rimmed glasses bobbing on an ovoid nose, leaving a rooster tail of water as he, once again, ran for cover.

I learned a lot about limnology from George in the college courses he taught, but most of what I learned was during conversations like this one in his small cluttered office on the third floor of an old building on campus.

And despite all the book learning and fieldwork, the image of this large man running lonely for his life on a small lake of ice and the notion that hard water won't stay hard, not forever, is lesson-worthy.

Each winter when I edge onto a frozen lake for the first time with a bucket and a can of wax worms, it cautions me.

I thank George for that.

Big River, Empty Road

Before my source at the tackle shop said it was fishable, I drove upstream along the river from St. Maries following the long, narrow stretch of forest highway.

In late winter, ice chocks the St. Joe and when the snow melts the river churns turbid and often rushes over its banks.

As I headed upstream, I met no other vehicle on the ribbon of pavement that heads into the Bitterroot Mountains that Idaho shares with Montana.

I passed an oxbow and flooded fields, the intersection to a once rambling mill town, and a series of railroad sidings whose names are only in library books.

Another town, its mill razed. A sawdust burner, once rusted along the river, gone too.

I passed a shuttered tavern by a green, iron bridge. The former proprietor, "the Greek," once took breakfast orders via CB radio here. He fed log truckers eggs, greasy sausage, and coffee, and the upholstery of the round stools, worn from years of hard use, were mended with duct tape.

A rip-roaring Marble Creek edged over its banks, its sheeny green water was the color of a cutthroat trout. I trundled on, passing nobody.

The sun stabbed through trees and slipped down rock ledges near Hoyt Flats where the doors of the ranger station were locked. Grass was snow-spotted but lush and the occasional bird shadow winged over the road.

A couple of pickup trucks with mud-speckled fenders were parked in front of the Avery Trading Post, the place that served burgers and let you gander at the skeleton of a man who according to legend, myth, or jocularity got stuck in a bear trap big as a toilet seat and died. Someone — again according to lore — painstakingly carried out his bleached remains and left them on the bar. Likely a fair trade for hootch.

High up in sunny meadows balsamroot, yellow as butter, nodded in a breeze sharp as an adz. Their flowery faces were the childhood memories of mothers, washtubs, and spring bouquets.

For a moment the day was a linotype, with a distant steam whistle and a dancing bear on a rope — all the stuff you read about this place from a century ago — but the road now followed an old Forest Service mule trail that was long covered with asphalt and lined with the riprap that buried a series of fishing holes.

I kept going.

Somewhere beyond Packsaddle near another campsite — its location was chosen for flat land wide enough to pitch a couple of tents against the river bank — I met a person on the shoulder bearing downstream with a fly rod. He wore an excited expression, a Turck's tarantula was hooked into a rod guide.

I recognized him as a kid who sacked groceries at a store in town, and I knew I was getting close to something.

I drove on as a spurt of rain fell from a cloud burst before the sun shined brightly again.

The trees made a tunnel in places. Spring clearing crews had scraped rocks and fallen snags from the road, gouging the pavement.

At a campsite just off the highway before a bridge, a handful of miles from the Montana border I found an old Ford parked in the trees.

I pulled alongside and got out of my car. The river was loud. It boiled. I couldn't hear my door slam shut.

Near the water's edge were two men wearing ditch boots. They were out far enough from a wall of fir and cedar to complete furtive casts with 9-foot fly rods and one at a time, as I watched, they pulled fish from the roaring river.

The cutthroat trout bent their rods like witching sticks and then as if on a leash the fish flipped and jumped coming out of the roar, shaking sunlight.

I watched the men for a while.

They occasionally yelled at each other over the cymbal-like clash of the water without knowing I stood behind them in the mottled shadows as they pulled trout from soft spots along the bank.

In the fishing story, "The Intruder," Robert Traver remembered a secret fishing destination far out of the way. When he got there, he learned that someone had beaten him to the remote honey hole. Someone, a lot like himself, wanted to be away from the crowd to tackle his thoughts through the abeyance of a few hours of fishing.

I had driven more than 60 miles upstream that spring day to check on the river and hadn't even passed a logging truck, which was unusual in the forests of the Panhandle.

These men along the bank in a glade of trees, and the kid who had walked the road grinning, carrying a fly rod, were the only people for miles. They fished a stream they called their own for a day and it made them richer.

Feeling like the intruder, I turned around without the effort of troubling any of them with conversation.

I remember that day, usually in early spring, while I scrounge the garage for fly boxes, vests, and the tubes that carry three and four-piece rods. Or when I hear someone say the rivers are blown. And it's sunny like it was then, but there's that whiff of mountain duff in the air and a bite of snowmelt from somewhere.

Everyone has a memory they aren't aware of collecting and harboring until it recurs.

When I returned to town that day, I asked the owner of the local tackle shop what he knew of those guys way out there catching trout in a river that seemed much too high, with a current that seemed too strong to catch fish, along a road only recently snow and debris cleared.

He knew their names.

"They like the odds," he said. "And the conditions."

Early spring anglers prefer the isolation weeks before the first camp trailer, before the fields farther downstream fill with fire rings and drift boats on trailers.

They like the alone complemented by the roar of the water and the vast freshness of the season.

Everyone wants an empty road to a fishing destination. It's more than a nudge. In a world of digital grit like tallow on our tongues, it has become a necessity that says odds don't matter, only the roar of the water matters and the cold heft of sky in a day stunted by time. One that seizes your limbs and chills your skin like a plum.

Being out there is all that matters.

Each spring provides another chance to unlock something new.

Spring

Shakespeare On A Dump Run

I knew a girl who could pull more gear, stay awake at the
wheel longer, and generally out endure most of her peers
during the sleepless commercial fishing openers on the coast.

She wore her strawberry hair cropped, carried mariner
tattoos on each of her arms and she hopelessly smote a friend
of mine.

He tried to win her affection with long nocturnal drives in
a 1970s model luxury car that sported duct-taped upholstery.
He played host to bare-knuckle boxing matches around
campfires, and placed flowers in brown bottles he collected
and hung on a line like freshly-washed dungarees.

The two, however, parted.

Alas, I should add.

He lost his job on a logging crew after sleeping through the
horn-blasts from an early-morning crew bus. And not long
after, lost his final paycheck by leaving its cash folded like
fast-food napkins next to his sleeping bag near the glow of a

flickering community fire circle.

Fiends, it became apparent, were about.

The girl — her name was Clare like the county in Ireland — headed north on a seine boat into the swirling mist accompanied by the cutting dorsal fins of porpoises and Orcas, and the sputtering wings of surf scoters.

The twain never again met.

If Shakespeare were alive I would have called him.

Write about this pretty please, dear bard, sir.

It was however no tragedy. Not a Troilus and Cressida.

The tide rose and my pal, call him Thelonius, went out with it, over the rocky escarpments and the bristle-back sea stars. He drifted into the ocean. The Japanese current grabbed his vessel. He did a stint on a couple of processing boats as if holding to the memory of the tattooed girl with the strawberry hair, but then he let go and became a wildland firefighter. He eventually jumped from planes into what he called "gobblers," at the behest of the fire god known as Big Ernie, but that was years ago.

He lives in the mountains now, in drier climes, and seldom writes to me.

When he does, he doesn't mention the girl with strawberry hair who built a wooden sailboat, blew down the coast to Seattle where she married, and is likely pursuing a life in a suburb with a decent white-collar job and long sleeve shirts.

In spring, memories like this pop from blithe dirt like new flowers. Through the foggy lens of years, they may appear to outshine what came after.

This phenomenon is true with everything but winning lottery tickets.

Last weekend while spring cleaning, I loaded old tin hats, saw chains, leather shoulder pads, rusting saw bars, and dried caulk shoes into a bin with deflated crab buoys and scraps of seine net.

I found myself staring blankly into the rear-view mirror like the Robert Graves poem where he scans his features, mulls eternity, and then pops the clutch on the pickup truck.

"Perseverance, dear my lord, keeps honor bright," Shakespeare said.

I clunked down the road with my rusty mail on the way to the landfill. Then — alas, again — from the wooded bluff heard a turkey call. The cheerful gobble shattered melancholy.

I came back to myself, as another bard penned, felt the slate call in a side pocket, and remembered the real work, and what still needs to be done.

Jewelry In The Hen House

Ruby and topaz lace, emerald frizzle, gold bars.

His wife collects chickens like other women take to jewelry.

It isn't a bad thing. It just came on kind of suddenly.

He bought an Auricana rooster for her birthday and then splurged on their anniversary.

The hatchery catalog has been open to a certain page in a conspicuous manner for weeks, he said, so he started saving for a clutch of Ancona eggs. The breed is rare in the U.S., according to the catalog people, and fares well on scanty rations. These scrawny egg layers attack owls and fence with coyotes, so they should fit right in at the seven-acre poultry patch in the family's predator holler, the man studiously observed.

Just for the heck of it — he called it romantic — he dropped a fistful of dollars for a few Wyandottes. They are good, medium-weight fowl for small family flocks raised in rugged conditions, according to the official description in the poultry handler's guide — a small magazine his wife keeps under her pillow. Their combs do not freeze as easily as single combs and the hens make good mothers. Their fine disposition, attractive curves, and many color patterns make them a solid choice for fanciers and farmers alike.

He told me this, straight-faced over coffee that had gone cold because of my rapt attention at the change in his once-fiercely intractable demeanor.

"What was that breed again? Wyandottes?" I asked and noticed a flicker in his eye.

"Yeah, that's it," he replied and explained how the person in Georgia who raises the variety and ships chickens of all ages and in various stages of health, to 4-H members and farmers throughout the U.S. asked why he wanted that particular breed.

"Don't you already have enough chickens?" The chicken man asked.

That's when the telephone reception crackled like a boot on a pile of layer pellets. He simply couldn't stand this sort of interrogation. He had bought the farm a few miles from town so his family could enhance their city routine with a slice of country living. They added an old pickup truck with a plow to their fleet and a tractor with an iron seat.

He learned the chicken man was once an engineer who took to raising fowl at the behest of his wife, who had left her job as a chief financial officer because of a blue Andalusian.

"Watch out," the chicken man warned. "Passion for poultry can have unexpected results."

Paranoia among the husbandry crowd makes me nervous.

That was last year, of course, well before his Auricanas laid hundreds of blue, pink, and green eggs the color of pond water.

Before he got the barred rocks and the silver leghorns that guard his woodshed like yellow-eyed banshees. And before his children began waking in the middle of the night to rise from their feather beds and pull on his fingers with the words, "Daddy can you go out and check the chickens, I think I heard them fuss."

The words prompt him to adorn a pair of weather-beaten Romeo slippers and lumber into the starless night with his long underwear flap hanging open and a 16-gauge single-shot poking the misty after hours like a cow prod.

He checks the pens and inhales the odoriferous stew of chicken dung, pellets, and feathers. Shines a light at the puffed balls of birds on their roosts and the skittering barn mice in the straw before tottering back to the house to flop into bed and dream of drumsticks and gravy.

Twice there have been raccoons, but they were denied, he said.

It dawned on him the guy from Georgia might have a point.

This passion for Minorcas and Orpingtons may require him to build an addition onto the coop, with a few more runs and an egg room. He may need to take weeks off work to account for the construction, and head to Georgia to see what real poultry cultivation entails.

He scraped the chicken dip from his city shoes with a plastic latte straw.

"It's not a bad trade-off," he said. "Poultry instead of diamond earrings, pretty China, silverware, or a new car for that matter."

There was just one hangup.

"Every time I walk into the coop, they tell me what I am," he said. "They say I'm cheap, cheap, cheap."

Early Spring Ax Tossing Contest

A hatchet works. Or an ax, but certainly not a splitting maul.

It isn't for the lack of trying.

A splitting maul, when it turns in the air, is like an antique wagon wheel, cut loose and wobbling ferociously down a hill headed to the farm pond. It scatters chickens and pigs with its goading and malevolent sense of disease.

That is why those splintered antique wheels are often used as garden art surrounded by cedar yard bark, as they quietly melt into the earth unobtrusively, keeping out of trouble.

Once vogue among the ranch house clique were wagon wheel chandeliers purchased on eBay, bought at farm sales or just pilfered from aging neighbors. Sandblasted and heavily lacquered, they were fastened with lights and suspended — 85-pounds of metal and wood — directly over the dinner table.

Eating scalloped potatoes and ham on ceramic plates illuminated by the white light from the undusted bulbs of wagon wheel chandeliers somewhat anxiously calls to mind the last supper.

For a throwing tool — because they are uncomely as wagon wheels — splitting mauls won't do.

Their unwieldiness, especially the nine-pounders, is purposeful. Mauls are made to drive through and split bolts of wood with brutish force and a full-body swing. Sticking surgically into a block of fir is not what splitting mauls do best.

Which is kind of the point of throwing an ax, or a slim and decisive hatchet, for wagers.

It's a game done best in a logging camp during spring break-up when days are coupled with static from a shop radio leaning against a window painted with dust.

Industriousness is defined by push brooms tentatively attached to long handles that roust grit and dirt from concrete shop floors that moments before were lavishly swept.

The logging shop in early spring is where a small contingent of loggers is often confined while waiting to be called back to the woods. Box end wrenches, big screwdrivers, and channel locks are wielded unacquaintedly as fondue forks. The content of dented lunch boxes — expertly repaired with staples or wire ropes from the mishaps they endured over the years — is the high spot of the day.

Monotony and the shop wage, considered a nice respite to keep the crew out of trouble, is no panacea.

It will happen. It always does at least once and sometimes more often, that one or two wrench turners will quite suddenly and inexplicably notice the many axes, hatchets, and splitting mauls leaning in corners, lying on benches and tucked behind the seats of crew cab pickup trucks.

Files and grinding wheels, flat stones and something to test the sharpness of a blade are astoundingly accessible.

Coincidentally blocks of wood large enough for an ax-throwing target lie in steaming piles outside under sun-melting snow.

The combination starts to itch at first before it transforms into a proposition.

"I bet ya 10 bucks I can stick this double bit in that cedar butt right over there."

A certain stance must be adhered to when throwing a shop ax or a hatchet toward the end of a cedar log. It takes a few tries to master.

If cedar prices are low the log decks include what loggers call pumpkins — big logs with fulsome ends — that beg for a bullseye to be sprayed on them with tree-marking paint. The contest may then pleasantly commence.

Rules are agreed upon and pointers are doled to contestants followed by jeers, chuckles, or laughs as throwers warm-up displaying a complete lack of prowess, or a dead eye.

Crafty contestants observe tight-lipped and expect the same when they cartwheel their hatchet or ax through the air and watch as it strikes a log face.

Glancing blows that careen wildly in some unanticipated direction are called unhealthy, which is pronounced "Ooooh," by the audience and may be followed by nervous laughs.

"I wouldn't be standin' over there fellah."

Participants quickly learn nuances.

Agile, long-handled camp axes throw differently than two-bit lopping axes, or short, wedge-driving hatchets.

When the newly honed implements find their mark it is referred to as "hotdamn."

Exclamation marks are whimsically added.

Sharp axes stick as solidly as dull ones. And just because an ax is sent flying in one direction doesn't mean it won't bounce in another.

Always there is advice at an ax-tossing row.

"Might grab higher on the handle, Bub!" Or, "That'un almost hit the boss's truck."

Early spring in North Idaho often seeks a diversion. Throwing axes — not splitting mauls — may fit the bill.

Board games are a safe alternative to tossing sharp objects at log ends out of rank boredom. Unless the playing table is lighted by an 85-pound wagon wheel chandelier.

With Murry And The Chena Ridge Dippers

When the wind blows, the Tanana River south of Fairbanks lets loose fine dirt that whirls into the sky like smoke from a quickly-moving fire.

The dirt is called loess and it rises and twirls far above the trees and can be seen miles away.

I saw it while sitting in the front room of the house where Joan and Niilo raised five children.

Niilo is an elderly man with a Santa Claus beard who prefers towels to slacks, especially on Sunday afternoons. He wraps the ivory-colored, fluffy-cotton beach variety around his midsection and the trend catches on with most people who visit Niilo's home on Chena Ridge southwest of the interior Alaskan capital.

I went to visit Niilo with a friend who jumps out of airplanes for a living. He gets paid for doing that, it's true, but his work isn't all that glamorous. After jumping out of airplanes he spends the rest of the time on the ground clubbing tongues of fire with brooms made of small spruce trees or gunny sacks filled with moss. That sort of thing.

He's a Bureau of Land Management smokejumper based at Fort Wainwright, and he pointed out to me the dust rising from the Tanana River.

"Every year we get calls from people who report a fire out there, but it's just the loess," he said.

My buddy Murry is the oldest working smokejumper in the U.S. He is pushing 60 and maybe that is why he visits Niilo and the people on Chena Ridge Sunday afternoons when he isn't fighting fires.

Niilo's is a bathhouse. It's come as you are, plop into the community tub, soak up the heat before dripping on the wooden floor and lounging around the kitchen table afterward, half naked, eating potato chips with a towel around your waist. The kitchen is where guests tell stories and invite you to share a few of your own.

Murry isn't a big chip guy, though. He comes for a hot bath and to talk with Niilo and Joan who are both in their 70s. He comes, he said, to relieve the muscle aches. He has stopped by the Chena Ridge bathhouse since the mid-1960s when, says Murry, all of Fairbanks was like one big construction camp.

Even before that, Joan and Niilo's was the only place that had running water on Chena Ridge. The water was plentiful and hot to boot. The couple wanted to spread their wealth around and offered their malodorous, ridge-tromping neighbors the luxury of a bath every Sunday.

"It was the only time a lot of them bathed," said one of the many people sitting around the kitchen table in the room with the low ceiling and a couple of wood stoves that had been converted to bookshelves.

A few towel-clad attorneys dripped at the round table in the kitchen. A couple of college professors joined the Sunday bath, a schoolteacher and a road boss who stripped in the living room and walked to the steaming tub room grumbling.

Some of the chip dippers asked Murry about the book he had written and he told them it would be on the shelves soon. The book, a sort of smoke jumper's biography called "Jumping Fire," was published by Harcourt, and it's a big deal.

The naked chip eaters at the table seemed impressed that my pal, Murr, Old Leathersack, had written and sold a book, but they didn't want to let on.

They had their own projects and erudition to pursue.

When the table talk turned to 16th-century nobility, Murry, who prefers conversations on land stewardship, fire ecology, or friendship, put his pants and boots on.

Fully clothed among the newly-clean, I returned the book that I had been perusing to a shelf and shook hands with Niilo who sat silently by the window overlooking the 160 acres he had homesteaded more than a half-century ago. He looked out from the ridge at the dust blowing from the Tanana River.

"That sure looks like smoke," I said because I didn't know what else to say.

"Just dust," he nodded, adding, "Every spring people think the forest is on fire."

A gracious guest, Niilo hugged Murry and invited us back. "The water's always warm," he said. "And there are plenty of towels."

For Public Land Gobblers, Bring A Mentor

A person turning left must yield to oncoming traffic, or the person turning right.

It's a simple traffic rule that too many people neglect, or don't know.

If you're the person turning right or going straight, and if you follow the rule, you'll often be greeted with the bird from a driver whose knowledge of rules is as twiggy as his manners.

The bird is the simple hand gesture of egregious cretons who don't know the rules, neglect them and abandon any pretense to neighborliness. Courtesy and rules are interchangeable.

A similar foul applies to chasing fowl — or any other game — afield, where courtesy and rules are often unwritten, handed down by mentors wearing wool, stout boots, and camo face paint.

Any novice hunter without a mentor would be well served to find one. All fine mentors instill the golden rule. It is as applicable in the woods as it is at the intersection by the shopping mall.

Being able to build a fire by rubbing sticks together isn't a prerequisite for a mentor because a butane lighter will do just fine, thankee very much. A mentor will have in his or her pocket a pouch of fire-building material that's waxy-dry and ready for a lesson on woodsmanship.

The state fish and game department rule book is also a prerequisite for novice hunters. Retrieve it from the moldy dip under the car seat and leaf through its neglected pages to the paragraph that starts, "No person may ... ."

Idaho is a rational state, unlike the autocracies from which many of its newly-minted inhabitants purport to hail. Courtesy and rules come down to what's sensible, such as don't harass game animals. Yield to others in the woods. And don't approach someone's decoys, blind, or stand to trade a golden sponge cake for a chocolate one with the creamy filling.

There is a time for that.

Know the time.

Mentors teach animal language, how to track, and how to read sign. They can expound at length on the fine art of scatology and when you both are sitting in a blind watching a flock of approaching turkeys your mentor will work magic on a slate call, or a mouth reed, or any number of Dr. Dolittle contraptions that allow communication with a medley of God's creation.

You must remain motionless. Mentors teach this lesson

sometimes with a hiss, under their breath. Let the rafter be the only thing moving, as long as it's coming toward you.

The spinning earth will move too, allowing the sun to rise in an arc over the wave-curves of the surrounding hills. And the lone ruffed grouse near the creek that thump, thump, thumps before whirring its wings in a frenzy seldom observed by mortals, will move as well, and that's OK. And maybe the field sparrows or a varied thrush in a bush spotted by sunlight will twitter.

But not you.

Or your mentor.

You are still as bark. A gun barrel points at your decoys. It rides the Y your knees make as they press, unmoving, together.

Yelp-yelp, cutt, cutt, purr, your mentor entices the flock of Merriam turkeys heading your way. The birds stop only for toms to glub, drag their wings, fan their tails, and dance famously like Oliver Hardy at a Decatur bourbon tasting.

These are the glorious days of spring your mentor has told you about. You've prepared by tucking two turkey tags into your vest, dropping the heavy twelve-gauge shells — the ones that pattern and have punch — into the deep pockets where they won't rub or click together. You painted your face ... Looky there. Where? I can't see you.

In a few minutes, you will cut your tag, high five your mentor, and admire the beard and fanned tail of your freshly-harvested quarry.

"Lookit them spurs!"

But wait a minute. What's this?

Sounds like a two-stroke engine. Nope. It's several two-stroke engines and they are farming the earth and getting louder as they till the soft, spring soil down by the creek and wet meadow you crossed in the dark to get here.

Oh. Oh.

You see them now gaily outfitted in reds and glow-green as they dart through the trees, speedily approaching the field, the edge of which you have staked as your own. And they rumble toward the turkeys that picked a path in your direction, until now.

The birds begin to putt loudly and chaotically as the toms fold their sails and, along with the hens, begin a slow trot toward the opposite tree line. Frantically their scrawny bird legs reach a lope, then a gallop. As the dirt bikes close the gap the gobblers kick grass, and the whole flock scampers full bore before taking wing like a bevy of herons. The motorbikes and four-wheelers, a growling and sputtering brick of firecrackers all lit to bang at once, explode in a voluminous chorus as their riders yeehaw and holler. The cacophony frightens the body fluids out of the busted turkeys making for a festive, rodeo hullabaloo.

When the fracas breaks over the hill and into the canyon, its clatter fading, and the gang of Merriam's glides into the next county, the only thing moving are the decoys in front of you. They silently nod in a breeze that stirs motorcycle exhaust like weak tea.

This is where a mentor comes in handy. Because instead of crying foul, or raising the bird in a hand gesture accompanied by the guttural howl that such a situation deserves, he or she remains completely undiscomfited.

Mentors have seen this sort of thing, likely many times. That is why they wear woolen undergarments, jackets, and pants. Their discomfort simulates a living, breathing purgatory.

They will turn to you eventually and smile. Ask to trade the golden sponge cake in their lunch sack for your small chocolate cake with its creamy filling.

It is time for that.

This unemotional composure that knows how to stymie hostility, salving the most ardent ill humor with a sugary snack, has won them the title of a mentor.

The Best Bird Dogs Train Themselves

If a dissertation was required on how to pick a pup, I would bumble a higher degree in dog-owning.

Although I have picked a lot of pups, all but one of them for bird hunting, my choices have invariably been hard-headed pointing dogs that over time — an hour or two — turned the trainer into a trainee.

"Putty," they seem to snigger to themselves, starting at a very young age.

Some of the "how to train a bird dog" books in my library say this is OK. As long as the result is a dog fluent in basic communication and one that lovingly performs the sit, fetch, down, drop, and whoa commands.

Cussing, dirt kicking, boorish threats, and lack of composure are listed in the index under how never to act in front of your dog.

If there's one thing training a dog will teach an owner, it's patience. All of the books in my dog training library recite this proverb ad nauseam.

I use the term library loosely.

My dog training library is a cardboard box on a high shelf in the garage where the books are layered according to the year they were tossed into the box.

I have not yet found the book that says my methods are worth the price of a bag of popcorn, and my dog is still waiting for me to learn patience, testing me every day, then skulking away as if to reconsider his training methods.

He has taught me to give him treats in the kitchen, and to allow him to coyly climb onto the bed in the morning to lick momma's face until she yells, "Get Out!"

He has taught me to allow him, after much training, to leap up and down the stairs, back and forth, back and forth covering three levels from the living room to the basement, gazelle-like but loud as a rhino. He has trained me to let him jump over furniture as long as he doesn't knock over the lamps, and to bark and keen like a pack of hyenas with his feet on the coffee table while glaring out the window at neighbor dogs pulling their owners briskly through the streets.

And he has been allowed to vent after hours of playing monkey in the middle by finally catching and then eating an entire Frisbee — sneaking up on it while it basks on the porch table unattended.

His teaching of course extends to the field — the most religious and significant of all arenas.

It is here in the draws, ditches, and swales along the edges of cut wheat, hay, or the rushes and swamp grass of marsh meadows that he has taught himself to hunt.

One of his most gratifying, self-learned techniques is the hold.

When he smells a bird, he stops.

His tail shoots out but he does not sally forth. His nose and tail are on the same plane, slightly tipped, and unless the bird moves he holds this position until snow, sleet, or, next summer's pool party begs me to reel him in.

Mostly, he holds point until I can waddle to wherever he is, which for me can take a while.

In part, because the dog is a mile away.

It is for this point and hold, the stoic position of his breed, the staunch intentness, the bristle of ruff and the complete self-control by a dog that would drag a roast off the counter in a heartbeat if he didn't fear harsh language, that I admire him.

He taught himself to do this.

Maybe his genes prevent him from doing otherwise.

In company, of course, I take credit.

"Man, I wish my dog would hold like that," a pal said.

He used a whoa table to teach his dog to hold, an aluminum tube with a leash drawn through it to keep his dog at heel, bells, whistles, clappers, and a steel collar with spikes on the inside for control, but his dog continues to blissfully flush and chase birds across the county like a spring wind.

"How did you do it?" My friend asked.

"Resolve mostly," I sputtered.

It takes discipline and academics, I crooned while

graciously offering him a book from my library.

Please accept this bit of pedagogy, I insisted. It appears you need it.

Sure, he said, do you have more?

A whole box, I told him.

Keep in mind, I said. There's one thing that is incredibly difficult to teach. It's a lesson not found in books and frankly ...

I paused here for effect.

I'm not sure that you're a good candidate, I sighed.

He considered the severity of what would come next.

Patience, I explained. It takes a lot of patience to train a dog like that.

Backroads, Pickup Trucks And Prine

There are truck songs and then there are pickup truck songs.

Truck songs for a time were about kids talking to long-haulers on CB radios and bandits being chased by Smokey through valleys called hollers, and a little bit of hotrod Lincoln thrown in to settle the matter.

Those days are treasured by some, but honestly, I can take them or leave them, like the hot beef sandwich and brown gravy at the Crossroads Cafe in Umatilla.

They are partially palatable but don't necessarily sit well.

Pickup truck songs are different.

They are the songs that click in the cab stereo when the elk calling cassette tape is removed, or they replace "How to Better Call Tom Turkeys in Five Easy Steps."

Willie Nelson, who to my knowledge did not take up the trucker song banner, but made a career of pickup truck songs, was once a favorite gravel-road balladeer.

A person could drive from the border of Montana, through a bunch of sneaky back roads and mountain passes, sometimes dodging green logging trucks, without removing Red Headed Stranger from the dashboard stereo.

Oh, Merle is there too, quietly crooning about his troubled past, and probably Johnny Cash, whose popularity was reinvigorated around the time Merriam turkeys were pushed through the pipeline and made a strong showing in the highlands around Lewiston, Idaho.

When tables turned to CDs Dwight Yoakum was singing Bakersfield with Buck Owens and farther back in the jockey box, behind the busted box call and a leaking bottle of cow elk urine is a Jackson Brown or John Cougar CD.

Add them to the list of tunes that knocked around in cabs of the Fords and Chevys, the small Toyotas and fat-tire Mazdas, the Nissan grinders whose transmissions wound up like a Jack-in-the-box under the bench seat while tooling backroads waiting for a deer to cross.

There was another balladeer though whose songs lived closer than inside the cab of a pickup truck.

John Prine's songs were memorized like only kids can memorize a song. Easily. They made immediate sense and every word was hung on the rearview like a tattered dream catcher.

When there was no stereo, or no John Prine cassette or CDs could be fished from the glove box or from under the seat, the songs were in your head.

My kids learned a song called "Paradise" at bedtime. It was

naturally melodic and as necessary as a glass of water.

They referred to the song as "Muhlenberg County" and would yelp, "Sing Muhlenberg County, dad!" often inside the pickup truck on snaky gravel roads winding under pines and tamarack that scratched the sky like a cat's belly.

When the CD clicked and the first guitar chords hummed as a bow slid over the strings of a fiddle their heads popped up like tarts, even in sleep.

"When I was a child my family would travel," they would peep rubbing their eyes, "...down to western Kentucky where my parents were born."

One of them at two years old could only be consoled on a trip to Missoula by hearing "Sam Stone" over and over again. She is 23 now and whenever we travel east, around Tarkio, Montana, the song finds a place in my head.

A friend of mine who saw Prine perform at the Mother Lode Theater in Butte, came away calling the musician a friend. John Prine had the same effect on millions.

When he died this week the newspapers called him celebrated, and he was, despite having spent a career moving along the back roads where pickup trucks lived.

His fans liked it like that.

Even if we want more, it's settling to know John Prine has left us with enough music and lyrics to keep us going for years.

It was time, I guess, that he dragged his saddle into the rain.

Spring Fishing In Montucky

Our guide Sancho carefully drew a map in the air with his index finger, uttering words that cause fly anglers to scratch their chins with a measure of dignity, before scratching themselves.

He spoke quietly of off-color water, of salmon flies, and big rivers. He self-consciously pontificated about spring creeks, rubber rafts, and tailwaters, backroads, cutoffs, and weather, then left it all hanging fog-like, this menagerie of words and geography, while we discussed among ourselves.

It was spring in Montana and if the fishing didn't hook you, the pulled pork sandwiches would.

From our starting point in an established neighborhood — as the real estate magazines like to call places with mature trees and grossly outdated homes — in arguably the most Western of Montana cities named for copper king graveyards and geological features that are a tribute to the Charlie Russell country to the north, we loaded up the carry-all and drove south and east.

Pronghorns grazed in this land of fences, cottonwoods, and gurgling streams.

The vista was conducive to historical reflection unless you live here and then you just pony up, ask politely for a beer, tip the bill of your ball cap with a forefinger, and wonder if you've got enough rubber leg bugs for everyone.

"How about a cold one?" You might say, as you press your flip-flopped toes against parking lot dust along a shadowy river, one hand probing the contents of an ice chest. "There's gotta be one colder than this."

We drove over a mountain pass and under one too, swept grand curves listening to newer versions of John Prine like those that got the crowd stomping at the Mother Lode Theatre several years ago, and we stopped in a place where a young guide named Cracker, a cross between your doctor and the kid who cuts your grass, sat behind a counter with one hand on the cash register and another on your self-image.

We bought a handful of flies and a few sundry items we forgot to bring along in the many hours of preparation for the few hours of fishing on a river called Ruby.

"Where you headed?" Cracker asked.

We told him.

"That should be fishing fine," he said. "The bugs in that bin have been heavy hitters."

Okay, we said and fondled a few.

"You from around here, or out of state?" Cracker asked.

The customers whose shoulders we brushed in the doorway carried sacks of fly fishing shirts, straw sombreros, and fleece-lined undergarments with the price tags flapping in a breeze to their BMW with Florida plates, they were from out-of-state by any measure. We considered ourselves from a neighboring state. One that has its own gold medal fisheries, as well as its own ties to hilljacks and trout.

"Idaho," we said, but he was unimpressed.

"Welcome to Montucky," he mused like a regular nineteen-year-old Milton.

He spooled line on a reel for us, intimating that neither the line nor the reel were worthy of our destination, and recommended some fly line hanging over there on the pegboard because it was pocked with microscopic craters that cut friction like moon boots and had a life expectancy of an elephant in the Bronx zoo.

"As much as you fish," he said. "You'd never have to buy another fly line."

We crooned. Fawned actually. Wow, we said, then wondered about its hundred dollar price tag.

Not that a hundred bucks is a bad deal for some outstanding fly line, but we had thirty dollars and a few balls of lint between us, pooled for hand-crafted burritos at a caravan in Dillon if we made it there.

We purchased a set of out-of-state fishing licenses, Cracker bade us good luck, and we said thanks, thinking we already had it. Mainly because our guide had a name grounded in the hallowed halls of literature, not alt-rock, nor the self-indulgent neck tattoos of the new world as the bell above the door went ting-a-ling. Heading deeper into the land of milk and honey, our fly rods were now fully loaded and strapped to the hood like harpoons.

"That sounded like a superb floating line," we said as we headed south.

"It's crap," said Sancho, who had one hand on a sweating bottle of brew and the other lacing a wading shoe, the steering wheel neatly tucked into his lap.

"Ridiculous!" he moaned.

"You can get it for twenty bucks on eBay," he cried. "And don't worry about leaders," he continued. "I've got some twenty-pound mono. I don't want you all losing my rubber legs on brush and such."

We motored past historical markers and the place where a Kentucky Derby winner was foaled in 1886 or something. Sancho, ever a horse aficionado, said Spokane was the thoroughbred's name and the chestnut stallion was born in that round barn, over there.

If this seems absurdly redundant it probably is.

We had all been here on numerous occasions in various shades of inebriation, only today, we started the morning with tea and had resisted compulsion the night before to liquidate our limited assets in the fine taverns of this sterling state, so everything, from the horizon to the traction of the radials seemed awfully new.

Montana rocks on many levels, especially in summer.

Winters here suck. We get that too because there was a time when we lived here year-round, but for now, we enjoy what our pocketbooks afford us: Driving the sweetgrass backcountry looking for trout in June, or May, or sometimes February and on into the rest of the year — yes, October too — while we reside elsewhere in those months when even the mercury heads to the Galapagos.

We're here for fish and the weather is tick-tock, clouds and sunshine, back and forth and we walk trails to the river's edge and Sancho leaves us to catch fish on his own. When he returns we have made neat little dream catchers of fly line, flies and alders quilted them with backcasts, quaint contraptions netted with feathers from a sandhill crane and a robin's nest, and he scoffs.

We lose all of his titanium-head rubber-leg bugs and dig into our own stash for woolly worms and grasshopper patterns that we drown with lead sinkers and eventually we catch fish, big rainbows that run and jump and splash and Sancho starts sticking closer to us.

The day gets dark.

There is lightning, and thunder growls like a belly overhead.

Sancho hangs tight and pulls a bundle of pulled pork sandwiches from a backpack.

And beers.

We sit on the riverbank in the grass watching the sky.

Eat up for soon we will die, he says, but I have misunderstood.

"Kill these and let's sack some fish," he says.

Later, when the sky is dark and raindrops plop in the river like pennies, we trudge the trails back to our vehicle and later, sit around a pine table in a small house in Butte drinking icy suds and knocking down the rest of the pulled pork sandwiches. Sancho, his eyes droopy now and his face dark, his skin like saddle leather on a new saddle, corroborates the tall tales of the day.

He understands the necessity of this and for that we are grateful.

"That was a big fish," he says. "They were all big fish."

We feel blessed.

And we go to bed.